A Saga of Early California II

Eagle Woman

By Marian Sepulveda

ISBN: 978-0-692-93456-2

Published by Sepulveda House
Palm Desert, CA

Library of Congress Control Number: 2017913254

Book Design by

AquaZebra™
Web, Book & Print Design
www.AquaZebra.com

First Edition
First Printing, October 2017

Printed in the United States of America

ACKNOWLEDGMENTS

To my friends and readers of Where Eagles Dance who urged me to write a sequel. And to publisher Mark Anderson who has guided me on this wonderful journey from the first paper back. Most especially I wish to acknowledge Esther Harris for her careful proofreading and editing, and my first readers Patricia Lant and my ever supportive big sister Virginia Foster.

Volume I, Where Eagles Dance was first published without Esther Harris' editing. And was I embarrassed by all the errors we all missed. Even the computers proof reading program didn't find them all. Some of my first reviews took me to task.

Fortunately Create Space prints books only on demand so issuing a corrected copy was easily accomplished with the help of my publisher

Mark Anderson of AquaZebra Publishing.

And, lastly, to Brian Carolan who said, "I want to be a character in the sequel." I didn't think that was going to happen, but suddenly I needed this character, and I named him Brian. I drew the line though when he said he wanted to be on the cover.

Enjoy.

PREFACE

The year is 1876, a fateful one in the history of all indigenous tribes in America.

Yuma warrior Night Wolf is investigating reports of sheep ravaging Indian land. He rescues a young white woman being attacked by one of the herders, and takes her to the medicine woman known as Eagle Woman. There is instant attraction between the two.

The saga continues as Abigail Cassidy Butterfield, known to the local Indians as Eagle Woman, is now living the San Diego back country with her family. Although this story is a sequel to Where Eagles Dance, it also stands alone.

Abby is called on to help the local tribes retain their land from the encroachment of white settlers and squatters. By becoming an Indian Agent she helps to smooth the way for the surveyors who need to reestablish boundary markers that have disappeared over time.

Danger stalks the party of surveyors. A dangerous medicine man has taken over Abby's land, proclaiming it to be Indian land, and who poses a serious threat.

Once the survey is complete, Abby and family personally deliver it to President Ulysses S. Grant in Washington D.C.

But meanwhile, events are unfolding in Montana that will have disastrous consequences for all Indian tribes for many years to come. It will take all of Abby's Eagle powers to save her Kumeyaay people and her family.

Enjoy the drama, the romance, and a few light hearted moments along the way.

Come with me to early California as the saga of Eagle Woman continues.

1

Yuma warrior Night Wolf guided his pinto into a thick stand of brush at the edge of the stream where he would be concealed. He wore a sleeveless buckskin vest and buckskin pants; his only weapon was a large hunting knife strapped to his side. For several minutes he listened before he dismounted to allow his horse to drink.

In the distance he could hear the herd of sheep he was seeking. The Kupa band of Indians, who had lived on this land for centuries, had asked for his help. A large herd had been driven onto their land and was ravaging it. Any attempt to get the herders to leave had been rebuffed by men with rifles. He had come to investigate.

Once he felt safely concealed, he stretched out on the ground to drink from the clear water of the stream.

"No! Stop that!" He heard a woman's voice from up stream. "Let go, Kamen!" Night Wolf heard the fury in her voice.

"Come on," an accented voice wheedled. "They won't know. It's just us out here. Ow! You hit me!"

"Bastard! Let me go!"

Night Wolf moved toward the sound of ripping material and saw a man grab the front of a young woman's dress and rip it, leaving deep scratch marks on her chest.

The woman boxed his ears and was slapped hard across the face. Screaming in anger she fought back as the man tried to wrestle her to the ground, wrenching her left arm sharply, bringing further screams of pain and outrage.

In two long strides, Night Wolf grabbed the man by his long hair and yanked him away from the woman, then sent him sprawling face first into the muddy edge of the creek. Growling in anger, the young man glared up at Night Wolf, ready to attack. His mouth fell open in shock at the sight of a large Indian warrior standing over him, a hand on the hilt of his knife.

"Not hurt woman!" Night Wolf ordered in his broken English.

"She's mine!" the man said angrily, but his eyes were large with fear.

"No I ain't!" the woman protested.

"Go!" Night Wolf barked, stepping toward the young man threateningly, his hand still on the hilt of his knife.

"I'll get the Marshal!" Kamen yelled as he scrambled to his feet spitting and dripping mud. "He's over by our camp!"

When he was gone Night Wolf turned to the young woman expecting to see fear, but she only looked at him with open curiosity. He scowled at the sight of her sorry condition. She'd obviously been abused by this man before, and her left arm hung limply at her side.

"I am called Night Wolf," he told her, hoping to ease her fears. "Come, I take you to medicine woman."

The girl didn't resist as he led her to his horse, mounted, and taking her good arm swung her up behind him. She didn't hesitate to wrap that arm around his waist as he headed into the nearby hills.

"What is name?" he asked in his limited English.

"I'm Mandy," she said, and strangely she wasn't afraid of this Indian. Her father called them vermin infested heathens, but this man smelled of sage and a not unpleasant male musk.

"Medicine woman not far."

2

"**M**a!" Danny hollered breathlessly as he burst through the back door of the farm house.

Abby looked up from feeding nine month old Ellie her morning cereal. Half of which had been spilled onto her muslin dress. Her green eyes instantly alert.

"There's an Indian in the barn! And a white woman who looks bad hurt," he panted.

"Slow down, Danny. Why didn't they come to the house?"

"He said not to tell anyone they're out there, and to tell Eagle Woman to bring her medicine bag."

Abby wiped the cereal from Ellie's chin. "Stay here with her and Jay. And do as he said, don't tell anyone else they're here."

Four year old Jay was seated at the table feeding

himself as Abby grabbed up her medicine bag and headed for the barn.

It took a moment for her eyes to adjust to the gloom. She saw her old friend Night Wolf with a white girl who looked to be fifteen or sixteen, her dress torn, her face bruised and who was cradling her left arm in a sling.

"Night Wolf," she acknowledged. "What…," she broke off as she realized the young girl was familiar. "Mandy?"

"Cousin Abby?" the girl struggled to smile, equally surprised, but was obviously in a great deal of pain.

Abby looked to Night Wolf, who spoke to her in the language of the Kumeyaay since his English was limited. "A white man was beating her because she would not lie with him. I had come to that area to see for myself the sheep-men with their herd on Kupa land. And I took her from him."

"Kamen said he was calling the Marshall!" Mandy said, guessing what Night Wolf told her.

Abby removed the sling and carefully examined her injured arm to see if it was broken. "Who was he?" Abby asked. "Last I heard Aunt Louise said you and Tod had run away from home because of Uncle Jacob's whippings."

"We had to," Mandy said as tears streaked down her already dirty face. "We'd had enough of his praying over us for our sins, and for not doing our chores just right. He didn't like that I was turning into a woman. Tod hated him! When he said he was leaving I begged him to take me too."

She whimpered in pain as Abby checked the extent of her injury, aware Night Wolf was watching with a worried expression.

"We think the lawmen search for us, thinking I have stolen this woman," he told her in the language of her former family, the Kumeyaay.

"I don't think it's broken," she pronounced. "Badly sprained, so the sling is a good idea."

She began to clean and medicate the scratches on Mandy's chest, where fingernails had raked her flesh, and there was a cut on her lip where she had been struck.

"Come up to the house," she told them. "I'll get you something to eat."

"I can't be seen here," Night Wolf told her. "They will think I took her."

"Okay, you stay here. I'll send Danny down with food."

He nodded to show food was needed. Abby put an arm around Mandy as they headed for the house. She could tell by how dirty her dress was, her hair uncared for, that she had been badly mistreated.

"Oh, she's adorable," Mandy exclaimed when she saw Ellie's cereal-smeared face. "What's her name?"

"I named her for my mother, Ellen. We call her Ellie. You've met my adopted son Danny, and that handsome guy with the milk moustache is Jason Daniel Butterfield. We call him Jay."

"I...heard your parents were killed by Indians," Mandy said. "Pa said you were kidnapped by them. Is that where you met Night Wolf?"

Abby nodded as she put together two sandwiches plus a jar of lemonade. "Not kidnapped, but I'll tell you the story later. Danny, take this out to Night Wolf. He's a friend."

"He looks mean," Danny said, hesitating.

"He's a warrior, but I've known him for many years. If anyone comes looking, don't let them know he's here."

"Okay, Ma." Danny took the food and headed for the barn.

While Mandy ate, Abby drew her a bath and selected some clothes for her to wear. "Who was the man who hurt you?" Abby asked.

The girl winced at the memories. "After we ran

away, Tod and I came across some Basque sheep herders, who took us in. They fed us, treated us real nice. When they realized we'd run away, they said they knew where Tod could find work. That they'd hire me to cook and do their wash and stuff. They'd take good care of me, they said." Mandy's frown was full of bad memories.

"Once Tod was gone....they stopped being so nice." She set down her partly eaten sandwich, unable to take another bite. "They lived in a large tent because they had to move often with their sheep... and...they put up another small tent for me."

Tears gathered in her eyes as she stared unseeingly at her plate. "Each night...a different one came to my tent."

Abby's mouth dropped open in shock.

"When Night Wolf found me, the youngest brother, Kamen was following me while I gathered water cress. I was hoping to run away, but they always guarded me." Tears slid down her cheeks. "Kamen decided he didn't want to wait for his next turn and was going to have me right there. I was so mad I fought him! That riled him and he got mean."

Abby handed her a napkin to blot her tears.

"Then suddenly this tall Indian hauled him

off me and sent him sprawling into the mud. If I hadn't been so scared I'd have laughed…but, strangely, I wasn't afraid of Night Wolf. Kamen ran off, yelling that the Marshall would be after us. Accused him of kidnapping me." Mandy drew in a long breath. "Night Wolf put me on his horse, but I felt safe, even though I'd never been that close to an Indian before. Later he made a sling for my arm and said he'd take me to a medicine woman. He called you Eagle Women."

"That's my Indian name."

When Mandy had eaten, Abby let her bathe and put on the clean clothes. She looked like a different woman when she joined Abby in the kitchen, where she was cleaning Ellie's face, and Jay was busy doing some of the clean-up, washing his own bowl and putting away his cereal.

Abby became aware Mandy was staring at her with open curiosity.

"What?" Abby asked.

"Your hair. Those white streaks at your temples. You didn't have that before."

Abby's hand went self-consciously to one streak. "I call them wings. Eagle wings. When I became a medicine woman, there was a sacred ceremony where the ancient spirits either accept or reject you.

These are the signs of my acceptance, because I freed a trapped eagle."

"That is amazing. I want to hear all about it."

Danny rushed in the back door. "There's riders coming. Night Wolf said there's probably a Marshall looking for him for taking the girl."

"Is Night Wolf hidden?" Abby asked, worry lining her face as she looked out the window at five approaching riders. One wearing a badge.

"Yeah, he put his horse in one of the empty stalls and hid his gear. They won't find him," Danny told her, also watching the approaching men.

"I'll talk to them," Mandy said.

"No," Abby insisted. "They don't all need to hear what happened to you. Danny, go out and make them welcome. Help them water their horses, and themselves, and let them pick some apples. Ask just the Marshall to come inside."

"Okay, Ma."

She knew Danny was up to the challenge. After surviving by his wits when he was homeless in the often lawless city of Los Angeles, he would know how to handle the visitors.

While the men settled in to rest and enjoy the freshly picked apples, Abby opened the back door to invite the Marshall in. Just past middle age, the man looked to be an experienced lawman.

"Howdy, Miz Butterfield," he said, doffing his Stetson hat, "I'm Lew Barker. We're searching for an Indian who kidnapped a sheep herder's wife."

"Wife!" Mandy broke in, outraged, coming in from the parlor. "I wasn't married to any of those bastard sheep herders! And the Indian didn't kidnap me! He rescued me and brought me here to a medicine woman."

The Marshall held his hat against his chest. He could see Mandy's battered face and her arm in a sling. "I don't understand, ma'am. Etienne Zubiri, the oldest brother, said you're his wife."

"Come into the parlor, Marshall," Abby invited. "I'll get you some lemonade and Mandy can tell you what really happened. It's something those men outside don't need to hear."

Mandy led the man into the parlor and they sat, waiting for Abby to return with the Marshall's lemonade.

Ellie was trying to eat some crumbled biscuits on her highchair tray. "Jay, watch your sister," Abby said as she left the room, but sat where she could watch them both.

"Marshall," Abby said, starting the story. "This is Amanda Bristol. We call her Mandy."

"Bristol! Jacob Bristol's runaway daughter?" he asked, startled.

"Marshall," Mandy said evenly. "I left home with my brother because my father often beat us. We couldn't take no more. And I'm sixteen, I'm of age."

That calmed the man. "But…why would Zubiri say you was his wife?"

Mandy's face crumpled as she fought back tears. "Me an' Tod ran into the Zubiris, and they took us in. We worked for our keep for a few days, but when they sent Tod off to work at another camp, they said they'd pay me to do for them. Cook their meals, wash their clothes." Tears slid down her cheeks. "But that wasn't all they wanted. I had my own separate tent…" It took a moment for her to compose herself. "Then…they started coming to my tent at night…one of them…every night."

The Marshall's mouth fell open. "Etienne said you was married!"

"No, there was never no mention of marriage," Mandy hiccupped.

"Well…that's…that's…" the Marshall was suddenly speechless.

"Slavery?" Abby suggested. "She was guarded day and night so she couldn't leave."

"But, they said an Indian took you."

"An Indian rescued me. Kamen was supposed to be guarding me, but instead he wanted to…." Mandy couldn't finish. "Wanted to…But this Indian stepped out of the brush, knocked Kamen flat, and then brought me here, to the medicine woman." She looked at Abby, tears glistening in her eyes. "I didn't know she would be my cousin."

The Marshall sipped his lemonade, his brow furrowed in thought, sorting through his options. "Do you want to bring charges against the brothers?"

"Marshall Barker," Abby answered for her cousin. "If we do that it won't be long before everyone will know what happened to Mandy. And laws have never been friendly to women who bring such charges. That's why we asked you in here alone. She'd be ruined. In addition to what they did to her, they are grazing their sheep on Indian land."

"Well…maybe they don't know…"

"They know all right!" Mandy said bitterly. "I heard them talking about it. Laughing. And that's why the Indian was there that rescued me. The Kupa Indians called him to help them get rid of the sheep…which were even being turned loose in their vegetable gardens. Eating their food."

"That ain't right," Marshall Barker said. "I'll go back and have a talk with those brothers. Threaten them with jail if they don't move their herd." He stood up. "Thank you for the lemonade, ma'am," he said to Abby, but seemed uncomfortable when he looked at Mandy, knowing what had been done to her. "I just wish I could haul them in for what they did to you. But, I expect you're right about keeping it quiet. I won't be telling my men."

"Thank you, Marshall," Mandy said, tears still glistening in her eyes.

"If I should see your pa, what should I tell him?"

"Tell him I'm fine, I'm with my cousin, and I ain't never coming home!" She sounded so definite the Marshall could only nod his understanding as he went out.

Abby and Mandy followed him into the kitchen, watched from the doorway as the men mounted and headed back the way they had come.

When Abby looked at her cousin she saw tears streaming down her face. Putting her arms around her, Abby hugged her, careful of her injured arm.

"It's okay, Mandy, you're safe now."

"I'm pregnant!" Mandy blurted.

3

"Oh my," Abby scowled. That's….that's" There were no words. "Sometimes… the Indians can…"

"No!" Mandy said vehemently, wrapping her good arm protectively over her stomach. "I hate those four brothers, but I can't hate this baby. One of them was nicer than the others, Ander. I'd like to think it's his."

"Did they know?"

Mandy shook her head. "I only realized it a few days ago, and I was afraid of what they'd do when they found out. I was making plans to run away but they always watched me."

"Well, you're safe here. And, if you want to stay, I would be glad for your company and your help."

"You won't tell Pa I'm here?"

"He's the last person I would tell, though I

understand he's fallen from his fiery pulpit."

Mandy's mouth fell open in astonishment. "I don't believe that!"

"It's true. Someday I'll tell you the story about him kidnapping me from Los Angeles and taking me to his farm. The man who is now my husband, John Jay Butterfield, with the help of my adopted son Danny, came to my rescue." Abby smiled at the memory. "Your ma really lit into him when she realized he kept me tied up in the barn, only giving me bread and water, and always praying for my supposed sins."

"And…and Ma finally did it?"

"Yep, chewed him up real good. If you saw him now, you wouldn't believe the change."

"Hallelujah!"

"If you want, we can get word to your ma that you're safe, but you're welcome here for as long as you want to stay."

"What about your husband?"

"John Jay has gone to his family home in Utica, New York. His father has had a stroke so he's handling the family business, plus he's trying to prod those politicians in Washington to get off their fat back sides and pass the legislation and treaties our Indian Agents have been sending them for the past dozen years." Abby was scowling with frustration. "It's so sad for the tribes who wait for the promised lands and supplies, and teachers for their children. But because of that inaction, the governor of California has been giving some of those lands to white settlers."

"He can't do that, can he?"

"Since the Indians have never been given formal title to their ancestral lands, the governor feels he has every right to grant homesteads."

Abby was pacing as she talked. "Mandy, I can really use your help. I need to go to San Diego to see the head of the Indian Commission. But I need someone to help with the children. I have an Indian woman, Delfina, who will go with me, but she's never been to a town, and needs help."

"Oh, Abby, I'd be ever so grateful to stay with you and help any way I can."

"Thank you. Now I need to talk to Night Wolf. Will you keep an eye on the youngsters?"

"Of course. I've had lots of practice with my younger brothers and sisters." She reached out a hand toward Abby. "Will you help find Tod? I want to know that my brother is safe."

"I'll do what I can."

Danny came inside to help Mandy with the

youngsters, while Abby went out to the barn, finding Night Wolf pacing restlessly, his horse again ready to ride. He went to her immediately, studying her face. It had been several years since they'd last seen each other, since the night he returned her injured husband to her and vanished into the early morning mist.

"You look well, Eagle Woman," he said in the Kumeyaay language. "You are happy here?"

"Yes, Night Wolf, I am happy. I have three children, counting Danny, and the farm is doing well."

"Your man?"

"He's in New York. His father is ill, and he works for the Indians with the government," she said, noticing the subtle signs of aging in his sun-weathered face.

"The woman?" he asked, motioning toward the house.

"She is my cousin, and she will be staying here with me."

He seemed relieved to hear that, and Abby was surprised he truly seemed to care about Mandy.

"I would like to make war with those who mistreated her," he said with a scowl. "They also use Indian land for their sheep, with no care for the damage they do."

"I told the Marshall about that. And one of the brother's lied, said you'd kidnapped his wife."

"Wife!" Night Wolf was outraged.

"Mandy set him straight about that, and she told him how the brothers bragged about using Indian land for their sheep."

"Ah," Night Wolf said with satisfaction.

"She asked him not to tell the others what the brothers did to her, or her reputation would be ruined."

"Bah!" he spat, not understanding the white man's ways about such things.

"The Marshall will have a serious talk with them, about Mandy, and about the sheep, so I don't think the Kupa will have any more trouble."

"Is good."

"I'll be going to San Diego soon to see the Commissioner of Indian Affairs, and I'd like a way to get in touch with you in case I need your knowledge of what is happening on Indian lands."

Night Wolf nodded. "I will go to a small camp near the San Diego River. I have heard you know Til-pu and her husband Andres who live there."

"Yes, they work for the Hartnells. I delivered Til-pu's baby when it wouldn't come naturally."

"I heard of this. Andres can get word to me. I

will contact him so he will know. When do you go?"

"Probably in two weeks. I'll send a message to my friends the Champions, they have found a home I can use while I'm there. John Jay and I may buy it. The owners died recently, and everything has been left as it was, except for some family heirlooms."

A sound from the doorway of the barn took their attention, and they turned to see Mandy, who had eyes only for Night Wolf. "Danny's watching the young 'uns," she said in a rush to explain. "I… wanted to see Night Wolf before he left."

With no more to say to Night Wolf, Abby walked away, smiling to herself. Something had happened between those two.

Years ago, Abby had left her Indian family to marry James Cassidy, even knowing Night Wolf planned to ask for her as his wife when he came next from the big river. And since then, he had never taken a wife.

She had known her destiny lay elsewhere. As a medicine woman, her visions told her she would help her Indian family more from the White world. After Cassidy was killed, she was kidnapped by Indian renegades who had stolen the horses of the Butterfield Overland Mail. One of the painted warriors turned out to be Night Wolf, who had intended only to steal horses, and had not intended for her husband to die.

Eventually he returned her to her Kumeyaay family, his plan to make her his wife again thwarted when a small pox epidemic devastated her village. As a white medicine woman, Abby knew how to contain the disease.

The village had barely recovered from that when a local rancher stampeded his cattle thru the village, grinding their ewa dwellings, their food, and most possessions into dust. Fortunately no one was killed.

It was then Abby knew she had to return to the white world to fight to save her people.

Years before, she had fallen in love with John Jay Butterfield from the first moment she saw him at Seven Springs Stage Station. Her husband was the station master. Though she wanted to love Cassidy, it never happened. And she could only love John Jay from a distance, knowing her feelings were reciprocated, but neither would act on those feelings.

After Cassidy was killed, John Jay had followed the trail of Abby and the stolen horses into Mexico.

Eventually Night Wolf and Abby escaped the plans of his cohorts to kill him, take his share of the money, and keep Abby. Night Wolf took her back to her people.

John Jay barely escaped Mexico with his life when attacked by Yaqui Indians. He thought he had lost Abby for good, only to learn she was in Los Angeles, hoping to help her people.

Danny came to her rescue when her employer had nefarious plans for her, then later helped John Jay track her to her uncle's ranch in Temecula. This led to the three of them becoming a family, which had now grown to five.

Night Wolf had loved her, and once she had been attracted to him. But it was not meant to be.

And what Abby had just witnessed in her barn between Night Wolf and Mandy made her smile. Mandy's baby would make no difference to Night Wolf. Indians looked at things differently than a white man would. There was no stigma to an out of wedlock child.

4

Abby was in her garden, picking tomatoes and peas for dinner when she heard a wagon approaching. She took off her apron, folded the vegetables into it, and set them on the back steps. Rounding the house to the front hitch rail, she recognized Judge Isaac Hayes from Los Angeles, a man she knew was dedicated to helping the Californios, as the original Spanish and Mexican families were called.

After Cassidy's friend John Rains was killed by Indians in Arizona on the cattle drive, the Judge had done everything he could to keep Rains' wife Merced from being evicted from the rancho that had been her father's. When she married John Rains, it then became his. Women weren't allowed to own property. Rains had then borrowed so heavily against the rancho that creditors were threatening to take it. Judge Hayes had stalled them until Merced made a hasty marriage to a man who could save her property. He also turned out to be a good man, and Merced and her children were well looked after.

Abby greeted the Judge and his driver, a young black man who assisted the judge in his work. Though no longer on the bench, Judge Hayes was still active in the affairs of California. He stepped down from the carriage stiffly.

"I'm getting too old for this," he groused with an attempt to smile as Abby gave him a quick hug.

"Come inside," Abby invited. "I'll get you some fresh apple cider."

"Ah, that sounds good."

"Joseph, will you join us?" she invited the young driver.

"If you don't mind Miz Butterfield, I see Danny down by the barn. I'd like to go say hello."

"By all means," she said.

She escorted the Judge into the parlor and almost at once Delfina came in with a tray holding glasses of apple cider and a pitcher half full.

"Vicenta sends her love," he said. "All goes well at the Carrillo Rancho. The young 'uns are sprouting like weeds."

Abby laughed. "She's fortunate to have so much

help. Her rancho is huge."

"Yes, and sheep's wool prices are up, plus they have alfalfa and orchards. With her oldest son to run things, she's been very fortunate to fare so well after Ramon's death."

"And Merced?" Abby asked, her frown showing her concern for her friend.

"As well as can be expected. Her new husband has been able to satisfy some of John's creditors, and he's allowing Merced to teach him how to run the rancho. Too bad John didn't allow her to do that. I guess he really made a mess of things." He took a long drink of the cider.

"I'm glad she found a good man," Abby said. "Though I understand you had a lot to do with that match."

"Yes, I've known Archer for many years. His father ran a mercantile store near Temecula, but was a poor businessman. Archer tried to help but the stubborn old fool wouldn't listen right up to the day he died. Thank goodness Archer is a smart man, with a good business sense. Good enough that he didn't try to stop the foreclosure on the store. He had some money of his own, but knew it couldn't save the mess his father made of things."

"I hope Merced will find happiness," Abby said wistfully, remembering her own marriage to James Cassidy. A man she had never been able to love. Though he'd been a good husband, she had never found satisfaction in their marriage bed. Not until John Jay Butterfield came into her life did she experience the passion missing from her life.

"What do you hear from John Jay?" the judge asked.

"His father is bedridden and failing."

The judge shook his head sympathetically. "Sad. And how about his visits to President Grant?"

"It's strange," Abby said with a deep frown. "All the dispatches that the California Indian Agents have been sending to Congress for approval can't be found."

"What? But....there are dozens waiting for approval. I helped write some of them. The Indians have been promised food, and teachers for their children, and a lot of other things that have never showed up." The judge was outraged. "How can they lose all of them? Maybe one or two, but all?"

"All," Abby repeated. "The President has been raising holy hell with Congress but it hasn't helped."

"So now what, I wonder," the judge mused.

"I'm going to San Diego to visit the Commissioner of Indian Affairs in two weeks. John Jay said the President has ordered a new survey in the San Diego mountains so the boundaries for the reservations will be clearly marked. But I also understand the governor has been granting land to settlers on what has always been designated as Indian land."

Judge Hayes shook his head in dismay. "Then it's a good thing I brought you what I did. It will help you with the Commissioner."

The judge opened his satchel and drew out a sheaf of papers. "I have a friend at the Capitol who I asked to gather this information. It's a report on all the laws the California Legislature has passed regarding Indians, not just here but for all of California."

"I understand many tribes have lost all their land in Northern California."

"They had the misfortune to hold lands in or near the gold fields. Many were run off, some slaughtered, some worked like slaves," the judge said. "At least our local tribes haven't been faced with that."

"I'll be happy to look at this information before I see the Commissioner. Now, I hope you are planning to spend the night. We have a nice guest room."

"I was hoping for an invitation, then we'll head back to Los Angeles in the morning."

Abby could hardly wait until they'd eaten dinner and the children had been put to bed. The judge had retired early, and Joseph had been happy to spend the night in the bunkhouse with the vaqueros. Once she was in her night clothes, Abby propped herself up with pillows on her bed and picked up the report the judge had brought.

The legislation went back as far as 1850, but before she could go on there was a soft rap on her door. "Come in," she called.

Danny entered, wearing a pair of long pajamas Abby had made for him.

"Danny, you should be in bed," she scolded, but she wasn't upset, he clearly had something on his mind.

"It's early for me," he said eying the report on her lap. "And…I was curious."

She motioned for him to sit on the overstuffed chair next to her bed. Over the years, she had been tutoring him just as Peter Wesley had tutored her during her years at the Seven Springs Stage Station, and her marriage to James Cassidy.

"Okay," she said. "Let's make this like a history lesson."

Danny grinned as he settled down to listen. He'd always enjoyed her lessons, even now. At the age of sixteen, he was grateful to have been officially adopted by the Butterfields. After his parents died of small pox, he'd spent several years homeless in the streets of Los Angeles. When he helped John Jay recover Abby after her kidnapping by her bible thumping uncle, he'd become family.

"Okay," Abby started in her best school marm voice. "When did California become a state?"

Danny's grin showed he knew the answer. "After a long debate in Congress whether California would be a free state or a slave state, it was finally admitted to the Union as free, in September 1850. The 31st state."

"Very good, you've been paying attention. Around then, gold had been discovered on the American River and that started the Gold Rush, and probably hastened the admittance of the state to the Union."

"And brought people running from all over the country to strike it rich!" Danny added.

"But those would-be miners found Indian tribes living peacefully along the river, which led to a lot of bloodshed."

Danny grimaced. He'd long since come to respect the traditions and culture of the local Indians after Abby's experience of being raised by the Kumeyaay. Her parents had been killed in an attack on their wagon train. Abby was thought to be the lone survivor.

"So what did Judge Hayes bring you? Something about Indian policy?"

"If I'm going to fight for the rights of the local Indians, I need to be armed with the history of the state's rulings, going back to the conflict in the gold fields."

Danny scowled. "I saw a lot of gold fever in Los Angeles. Men went plumb crazy trying to get space on sailing ships or stage coaches headed north."

"According to this," Abby said. "The state of California, already in 1850, had passed an Act for the Government and Protection of Indians… which facilitated their removal from their traditional lands, and further separated a generation of children from their families, their language and their culture."

"Why?" Danny demanded, startled the Governor would enact such a policy.

"That's not all," Abby said, scowling at the papers in her hands as if they were red hot. "There was a California law that provided for apprenticing or indenturing of Indian children and even adults to Whites. Plus lawmen could punish vagrant Indians by selling them to the highest bidder at public auction, to pay their fines."

"I saw that when I was in Los Angeles but I didn't understand what they were doing. That sounds like slavery to me…only with Indians instead of Blacks."

"And that's only the start. The Indians in Northern California fared far worse than our local tribes, or clans as they sometimes call themselves."

"But squatters are still taking over Indian land and calling for troops if the Indians object," Danny added.

"County courts determined which Indians and which children were to be apprenticed…or indentured. And under the State Militia Laws, the governor could order local sheriffs to conduct expeditions against the Indians."

"Slaughter, they mean," Danny said, thoroughly aroused by what he was learning.

"Between 1851 and 1852, eighteen treaties were negotiated with California Indians, and not one has ever been ratified."

"Nothing has changed," Danny said. "Pa said

they can't find any record of those treaties or the ones our local Indian Agents have sent recently. They've plumb disappeared."

Abby read on. Over the years, legislative acts nearly decimated some Northern tribes, which seemed to be the whole idea behind them. Indians had no rights. They couldn't vote, no white man could be convicted of any offense based on the complaint of an Indian. In other words, Indians had no legal rights regardless of the situation. And punishment of an Indian could be meted out by any complainant…in any manner he saw fit.

"Because of the indenture-apprentice laws, some Indians were kidnapped. In some cases, Indian parents were killed so their children could be sold for profit," Abby read.

"It's no wonder the Indians have tried to fight back," Danny said with a scowl.

"Only to draw the militia," Abby added, mourning for all the families who had been ripped apart, without recourse. "Even when treaties were signed locally, they were promptly ignored."

After Danny went off to bed, sleep was a long time coming for either of them. The plight of the Indians seemed to be a hopeless cause. But it was one Abby would do her best to rectify for the local tribes. At least they hadn't had to deal with white men with gold fever.

That night as Abby tossed fitfully in her bed, still upset by the report the Judge had brought, an eagle appeared in her dream. Below the eagle was a party of men mounted for a long trek, with supply-laden mules and some strange equipment. As they started on their trek into the mountains, she realized she was one of the party. Overhead the eagle flew along with them, as if keeping watch.

After that, she slept soundly.

5

Abby loved the small house she moved her family into in San Diego, only a short distance from the Champions, where she and Cassidy once stayed.

Violet Champion had become a good friend, welcoming her husband John Jay when they'd visited two years ago with Danny and two-year-old Jay.

The house showed a bit of wear and tear, but a lot of love had gone into the furnishings. There were linens and everything Abby needed to set up housekeeping.

Mandy helped get the two youngsters settled, while Danny set out to explore the neighborhood for mercantile and other services they might need.

Charles Champion called for Abby in his surrey to take her to the office of Judge Hartnell, whom she'd met before. It was at his home that she had delivered his Indian servant Til-Pu's baby. Her medicine woman knowledge had saved the lives of mother and infant, and earned the eternal gratitude of husband Andres, of the Inaja band, who swore he would one day repay her for the two lives she had saved.

"Abby, Abby," Judge Hartnell greeted her. "So good to see you again. Come in. Sit down."

Charles Champion sat in on the meeting as both men were well acquainted with the movers and shakers of the government in San Diego.

Abby settled into an upholstered chair, and rather than sit behind his desk the judge took another chair facing her, while Charles took a third one.

"I know you're here about problems with the Indian tribes in the mountains. Tell me what I can do to help."

"I need an introduction to the Indian Commissioner for this area. I've met with the local Indian Agent, but he hasn't the authority to help with what is happening in the mountains. There are squatters moving onto Indian lands, and sheep herders grazing their sheep there," Abby said, the depth of her feelings showing in her eyes.

The judge nodded. "I've been hearing of these complaints from Andres, Til-Pu's husband, and I think you're right. Something needs to be done before we start another Indian war. I'll arrange for you to meet with Commissioner Higby. Give me a day or two and I'll send word. I understand you're staying at the old Connor home."

"Yes," Abby said. "And I would very much appreciate your help setting up a meeting with the Commissioner."

Fortunately Commissioner Higby had heard of Abby and her life among the Kumeyaay, and readily agreed to a meeting. Abby had chosen to go alone into his office, with Danny remaining outside with the carriage.

"Mrs. Butterfield, it is an honor to make your acquaintance."

"Thank you, Commissioner. I can also say I've heard good things about you, and your attempt to help the local tribes."

"Please sit. Would you like some tea?"

A servant had come into the office so Abby accepted tea. When they were again alone, Abby had the feeling the man was truly glad to see her.

"You've heard about the problems in the mountains," Abby said. "The squatters on Indian land."

"Yes, yes I have, and I've been stymied by the fact that when I send my agents to make contact with the Indians, they're suddenly nowhere to be found."

"They don't trust you," Abby said. "The white man has rarely proved to be their friend."

"Because their main contact is with those who want their land. The biggest problem is that while Congress once set boundaries, most of them aren't marked. Or, if they were, the boundary markers have disappeared over time. The last official survey was when California was admitted to the Union. The entire state was surveyed, with ranchos and Indian areas marked." He gave a long sigh. "The Indians have always known their own boundaries, but we can't get them to talk to us."

Abby had an inkling of why the man had been so eager to meet with her.

"We've petitioned the United States Government to assign a certain section of land to the Indians, our agents make promises that the government doesn't keep. We just keep spinning our wheels." He sounded frustrated. "We make what proves to be empty promises. It's no wonder the tribes won't talk to us."

"I see your problem. I was hoping you would be able to send some surveyors to set legal boundaries, complete with official survey markers."

The Commissioner ran his hand over his thick,

graying hair. "And there's the problem. The tribes won't meet with us. We need someone they know and trust and can speak their language."

His intent look as he studied her frowning face gave Abby a hint of what was coming.

"I want to appoint you as temporary Indian Agent, to lead a party of surveyors into the mountains, make contact with the Indians and try to set the official boundaries. Ones the white men will be forced to acknowledge."

"You want me…?" for a moment she was stunned, then she remembered her dream.

"Who else could I send, Mrs. Butterfield? I've racked my brain, and you would be the answer to my prayers."

"Oh!" she gasped in surprise, but quickly saw what he was proposing was the only way it could work.

"I know you have Indian friends who would also know the area, who would be known to the tribes and speak their language. We would furnish all animals and supplies, and I have surveyors with their maps standing by. We have a copy of the original plats, which is what we call the maps, for this area, but over the years things have changed, boundary markers lost. A lot of land has changed hands as the Mexican Land Grant owners sell or lose their property."

Abby could barely process what he was saying, mentally planning how she could make this work. She would need Mandy more than ever with the children. And Danny, as man of the house. She had to make this work.

"I need to get a message to my husband," she said. "He's been working on the tribes' behalf in Washington, but not having much luck."

"Yes, we'll need his help there. We can send a telegram."

The Commissioner seemed to remember the cup of tea at his elbow and took a long drink of the now cooled liquid.

Abby did the same, needing a few minutes to consider everything such a trek would need to succeed.

The judge went on. "I've also heard you are an old friend of a certain Yuma Indian who is often in our area."

Abby's hand froze on the cup at her lips.

"I'm told the tribes in the area know him and respect him. Even though I'm certain he's done some things our ranchers take exception to, he could be a great help on this venture. Some call him El Lobo. Others call him Night Wolf."

Abby almost heaved a sigh of relief. "I know how to reach him," she said. "And I'm certain he will agree to go with us."

"Excellent. Excellent."

"And we also need the help of Judge Hartnell's Indian servant Andres. He also speaks many of the dialects Night Wolf or I do not."

"I'll speak to the judge." The Commissioner sat back in his chair, a look of relief on his face. "This situation has troubled me greatly. Let's say two weeks from today. Your party will leave from the site of the old mission."

As Abby returned to her temporary home, she knew she would send Danny, Mandy, and the children back to the farm at Eagles' Rest to await her return at the completion of the survey.

Danny was fully capable of managing the ranch with the help of the long-time foreman, Pete, who had worked for the former owner.

6

John Jay reread the telegram for a third time, trying to absorb the too brief message. Abby, an Indian Agent, sent to survey the mountain tribes' boundaries? He understood why his wife was chosen. She was the only one the Indians would trust. Arrangements were in place for the care of Jay and Ellie. He trusted Danny, plus there was Jacob's runaway daughter. If Abby trusted her with their children, then he would too. While she was in the back country, Abby would be out of touch.

He looked at his father, sleeping peacefully after he'd read the telegram to him. Partially paralyzed from a stroke, John Senior was barely able to speak, could not walk without assistance, but parts of his intellect were still intact, so John Jay kept him up to date on what was happening in Congress, and with the President.

Even though President Ulysses S. Grant knew Congress had not acted on any of the Indian Agents' promises, or acknowledged any laws passed by the Governor of California, he hadn't been able to prod them into action. Nor was there any explanation as to why none of those treaties and proposed laws could be found. Even the fury of the President hadn't been able to uncover what was lost.

Perhaps, with the boundaries set by the survey team Abby was accompanying, something could finally be done. Already land promised to various tribes had been given to homesteaders who were still arriving in California in droves in search of gold or free land to farm.

John Jay didn't envy Abby trying to make sense of it all, and wished he could be there with her on the hazardous undertaking. He was both relieved and concerned that Night Wolf would be part of the survey party. He knew the man had loved Abby, but still, the Yuma Indian had saved his life during the attack on the cattle drive. In Arizona, Yaqui Indians killed his friends John Rains and Ramon Carrillo. He, too, would have died under the hooves of the stampeding cattle if Night Wolf hadn't pulled him up onto his horse and carried him to safety.

Once safe, the warrior had tended to John Jay's bullet wound, and using Indian trails took him back across the desert to Abby. Though the Yuma warrior loved Abby, he knew she could not be part of his rebellion against the steady encroachment of white settlers on Indian land. She could better help the People from the White world.

"Jay Jay," came his father's weak struggle to get the words out. "A..Abby?"

"Yes," And John Jay told him again what the message said. He wouldn't remember their earlier conversation. "The committee is finally going to act on the Indian problem. They're working on a plan for reservations, and Abby is going with the survey party to reset boundary signs that have been lost over the years. That's going to be a bitch!"

John Senior nodded his approval. Then just listened as John Jay told of his latest visit to the Capitol, and a visit with one of the Under-Secretaries. It was not unusual for John Senior to fall asleep while his son talked.

7

The day was breezy and cool when the survey party left San Diego, heading into the backcountry where a number of Indian villages were scattered.

One day earlier, the cook with his equipment and helpers had set out on the trail to be ready for the main party when it arrived at the camp.

Night Wolf and Andres had gone ahead of them to contact any villages on the way. The cook, Bertram, had pack animals and five men to help him set up the evening camps. There were few wagon roads where they were going, so everything had to be packed on mules.

Abby rode with the surveyor, Jake Wilcox, his assistant Sunny Pritchart and five more helpers, a mixture of Indians and Mexicans, to convey the surveyors' equipment, and the stakes that would be used to mark boundaries for the reservations.

To Abby, it felt good to be in the mountains again. She was wearing a split riding skirt, long sleeved shirt and a hat with a string that tied under her chin. A kerchief was tied about her neck, and her red hair was braided in one long plait. Being the only woman on the trek didn't bother her. The Indian helpers were in awe of Eagle Woman, the Mexicans respectful.

"Have you been in these mountains before?" Abby asked Jake as she rode beside him.

"About a year ago I did some preliminary work, but without markers it wasn't easy to figure out boundaries," he said. A middle aged man with a slight paunch, Jake had seen his share of the back country. "Between the governor granting Indian land to settlers, and squatters picking a likely spot, not realizing the Indians had a prior claim…this won't be easy."

His gaze was set on the mountain trail ahead of them, his well-used hat pushed back on his thinning rust colored hair. "Uprooting those squatters is never easy. It will take a Marshall and a group of men to persuade them. It's not our job, other than to tell them they're on private land."

"I don't envy law enforcement that job," Abby

said. "If it's Indian land, they think they have a right to take it, and often, sheepherders will graze their flocks wherever they please, sometimes even on Indian crops."

On the second morning out, Abby went from her private tent to where a long table was set up by the mess tent. An array of foods were laid out for the men, most of whom were sitting on any convenient rocks or tree stumps, eating. A few had thought to bring canvas folding seats.

As she poured her coffee she saw Bertram, the cook, standing in the opening of the mess tent scratching his head and scowling.

"Something wrong, Bert?" Abby asked.

"I ain't sure," he said. "I don't think I misjudged how much food we'd be needing, I'm used to feeding hard working, hungry men. But I swear we're short."

"Short of what?" Abby asked, warming her hands on her coffee cup.

"Well, flour, beans, maybe tinned meat."

"So it's not animals," she said, considering what that could mean to their mission.

"Yesterday the same thing, but I thought I must have misjudged. We have to go easy if we're to have enough for the rest of our job."

Bertram went back into his tent, doing a recount.

Abby didn't think any more about it. There were scrambled eggs, bacon and biscuits for her breakfast, and she joined some of the men who were just finishing their breakfast, some going for seconds. Later, she rode out with Jake and his surveyors to take the day's measurements of a long valley before them.

The following morning when Abby went for breakfast, Bertram stepped out of his tent with some papers in his hand.

"Riley!" he called out. "Git over here!"

One of the men standing around the fire broke away from the group. "Yes, sir?"

"Are you sure you got all the food and supplies on this list?" he demanded.

"Oh, yes, sir. You can see my check marks. Everything you ordered was loaded on the mules."

Bertram's scowl deepened as he studied Riley's check marks. "I'd swear some of these supplies are missing."

"Can't be, sir," Riley said confidently. "I saw to the loading of the mules myself and they were never out of my sight."

Though Bertram was still scowling, he didn't dispute his top wrangler. "Okay," he mumbled.

"Thanks."

Riley refilled his coffee cup then joined his friends by the fire, while Bertram made preparations for breakfast, still frowning.

Later, as Abby took her plate of biscuits and gravy to a log at the edge of camp, she heard a distant bird call and a soft tred behind her in the brush. The sounds were familiar, not ones that alarmed her.

Night Wolf appeared. "You're being followed," he said without preamble. "They stay back, but always behind. Some days mules have heavy loads, other days small load. They visit local ranches to sell, I think."

"We're missing supplies," she told him.

"Ah," he grunted. "You have a snake in your midst."

"Yes, I'm afraid we do."

He vanished as quietly as he had come.

By the following morning the men were grumbling because breakfast was short rations.

"Short rations, Bert?" Abby question Bertram.

"I swear, Miz Butterfield, I know I ordered plenty of food, and I know some of it is missing."

One of the men overheard that statement and went immediately to tell the others.

"How can it be missing?" George Oakley demanded, storming over to Bertram and Abby.

Good food was one of the main inducements for a wilderness job such as this.

"You sure you ordered enough?" Luis demanded.

"I know he did," Riley said. "I saw it loaded on our mules, and when I look in the supply tent now, it don't look right to me. Some of it is gone."

The men were grumbling among themselves, getting angrier by the minute. They were a long way from any stores. There was no way to replace what was missing.

It was then Abby remembered Night Wolf's warning that they were being followed by men with mules. She went to where Jake was loading his surveying equipment onto mules, but he had paused when he heard angry voices coming from the camp.

"What's all the fuss, Miz Abby?"

"We're missing a lot of supplies," she told him

Before she could go on Bertram strode up to Jake. "We're missing enough that we can't complete our job."

"Night Wolf said we're being followed," she told them. "By men with mules."

Jake stormed around to the rear of the tent.

At first glance it seemed normal, but then a small wrinkle in one corner caught his eye.

Bertram, Riley, and several others watched as Jake moved up closer to examine the corner, finding finely stitched rawhide holding a long slit together.

"Son of a bitch!" Jake growled, then turned back sharply to the waiting men. "One of you knows about this! Line up, all of you!"

Hesitantly the men obeyed, forming a long uneasy line as the men looked at their companions suspiciously.

"Let me do this," Abby suggested.

Jake stared at her thoughtfully, then nodded before he turned back to the men. "We have a thief in our midst!" he yelled. "We're missing enough food that we can't complete our mission!"

He stormed up and down in front of the men, some of whom cringed under his withering glare. "We have with us a woman known to have a special gift. The Indians call her Eagle Woman! She will look into your faces, and she will know who the thief is!"

The men glared at each other, trying to guess which one looked guilty of stealing their food.

Abby was wearing her riding clothes, ready for the day's ride, when she stopped in front of the first man in line to look into his eyes. From somewhere inside her she felt the building of raw energy. Even though she was a bit rusty, it was something that allowed her to see into the man's heart.

She moved down the line, stopping before each man, looking into his eyes. Even though they fidgeted nervously she detected no guilt... a lot of anger to be under suspicion...defiance maybe, but no guilt. Until near the end. One man couldn't meet her eyes. Abby let her gaze focus on his nervous mannerisms, his shifty eyes and knew she had found their snake.

The other men realized it was one of their trusted companions, and even as the man turned to flee he was grabbed and held. The other men were furious. They would go hungry and no doubt not get full payment for work they couldn't complete.

Abby tried to calm the furious men but she was shoved away. Jake held her back as the violence erupted. A rope appeared and Abby was horrified to think they would hang the man. Half the crew wanted to string him up, but cooler heads prevailed and when they shoved him up against a tree, they tied him there.

"You better pray your friends find you, Diego," Riley growled as he stood back to glare at his former friend.

"Come on, Riley! Please!" Diego begged. But his words fell on deaf ears as the camp was broken down, loaded on mules and moved out.

Already Jake and his survey helpers were on their way to the next location, where he could set up his transit, and his Waywiser, a special wheel hitched to a mule used for measuring distance.

Abby rode on ahead to the Barona village to meet with some relatives of her Kumeyaay family. She found need of her medicine skills and she spent most of the day there. She also met with the elders to explain why the white men were in their area. As always, the Indians were skeptical of the white men's motives, but they trusted Eagle Woman and would spread the word to neighboring villages.

On her way back to that day's camp site, Night Wolf and Andres joined her.

"Your snake's friends found him," Night Wolf told her. "And they have turned back to San Diego. You won't be troubled by them again."

"He should feel fortunate they didn't hang him," Andres added.

"Some of them wanted to," Abby said.

For a time they rode together silently, but Abby

could tell there was something on Night Wolf's mind. She looked over at him, seeing that the young Yuma warrior she had once loved was now a mature warrior, a man whose dedication had changed from revenge on the white men, to helping his people, no matter what tribe.

In his eyes she saw the change, and had a feeling Mandy had something to do with it, and she smiled. "She'll be waiting when we get back," she told him.

"But…she is white. I am…" his voice faltered.

"A very good man, who deserves a woman who will love him with all her heart."

"You would accept this?" he seemed surprised.

"I will accept whatever Mandy wants, and I think she wants you."

"And a baby," he said with a look of wonder in his eyes. "I will be glad to be a father to her child."

Abby smiled happily, tears streaking her cheeks. "She couldn't find a better man."

8

The following evening, in the area of the Viejas village, Bertram had set up camp while Abby and the surveyors contacted the elders, explaining their mission to get a formal approval for their rights to the land, and place stakes to mark the boundaries.

Frustrated by the lack of supplies to feed them all, Bertram was looking at the meager remnants, enough flour for biscuits, a few tins of meat, some apples and corn, when the sound of hoof beats brought him out of the supply tent.

Night Wolf guided his horse close to the table set up for food preparation and dumped a freshly killed deer at Bertram's feet.

"Hallelujah!" Bertram cried. "Thank you, friend!"

With barely a nod, Night Wolf was gone. Bertram shouted to his helpers and they quickly set about preparing the fresh meat for the evening meal.

Abby was weary when she rode into camp with Jake and his men. It had not been easy to convince the Viejas village that their mission was to help them keep their land.

It didn't help her mood to realize this land had been granted earlier, though not legally. Because it was so rocky and hilly, there were limited areas for growing crops. It was land no white man would want.

She could smell the venison roasting, and knew someone had made a kill.

"Night Wolf," Bertram explained when Abby poured a flagon of water to erase the trail dust from her throat.

She wasn't surprised. Though she rarely saw him, she liked knowing he was near and looking after the group.

"We'll be at Green Valley tomorrow," she told him. "And you can buy supplies at the store in Cuyamaca. We'll be on my land, so we can set up a camp where we can stay for several days. The surveyors can do day trips to several villages from there."

"You own land up here?" Bertram asked with a look of surprise.

"My late husband, James Cassidy bought it, expecting to use it to grow wheat and other crops for the Overland mail horses and for the settlers coming through our Seven Springs camp." Abby drew in a long breath, remembering finding her husband dead while he tried to defend the Overland's horses. Both he and their good friend Peter Wesley died that day.

She tried to shake off the memories of the events that followed, when she was nearly raped before an angry Night Wolf killed her attackers and kidnapped her. They soon joined up with his cohorts and the missing horses, headed for Mexico.

It had been Night Wolf's intent to punish her for marrying a white man when she knew he would ask for her as his wife on his next visit. Following the massacre of everyone on her wagon train years earlier, including her parents, Abby lived with the Kumeyaay until she was old enough to marry.

But, in Mexico, Night Wolf soon realized they would both be in danger once they'd received the money and supplies for the stolen horses because the Yuma leader, Black Horse, wanted Night Wolf's share of the money, and his woman. They ended up fleeing for their lives.

Abby shook off the memories when Bertram's voice cut into her thoughts. "I'll be glad to stay in one place for a few days," Bertram said. "Breaking camp every day is a real pain."

"There's good water and a Kumeyaay village. Night Wolf has told them to expect us," Abby said, banishing the ghosts from her past.

The next day, as the group was on the move toward Green Valley, Abby was surprised when Night Wolf and Andres pulled up on either side of her horse. She could see by Night Wolf's expression that something was wrong.

"I have been to your people to tell them to expect you and all these white men, that you will want to stay for a time on their land--your land," he amended. "But there are others who have pushed your people out of their homes along the river and into the back country, and taken the best land for themselves."

Abby frowned, seeing his agitation. This was bad news. Night Wolf went on.

"I know of their leader, Sotero, who calls himself a medicine man. There are some renegades in his group, with their families."

"Did you speak with him?"

"Yes. I told him this was your land, and that

you and a large group of white men are on their way to make camp there." Night Wolf had to hold back his high-spirited pinto as he tossed his head and strained at the halter, not liking the noisy party of white men and supplies following them. "He said that has always been Indian land and you are not welcome. I told him if he made trouble the soldiers would come, because it is no longer their land, that Eagle Woman has legal right. You chose to share it with your people, the Kumeyaay, but he has no right to be there."

Abby was silent, wondering how to handle the situation.

Night Wolf went on. "Sotero considers himself a very powerful medicine man. Most Indios in the area fear him. You must be careful dealing with him. He's like the coyote who creeps up in the dark, stealing crops and animals. You must post guards while in the area."

Jake rode up on Night Wolf's other side, sensing the seriousness of the conversation. "Trouble?" he asked.

"Yes, my people's village has been taken over by renegades, forcing the Kumeyaay into the back country," she told him.

"Will they recognize your authority?"

Abby shook her head. "I've heard of Sotero. He can be very treacherous."

"He makes promises with one hand," Night Wolf said in Kumeyaay to Abby. "And then stabs you in the back with the other."

Abby translated for Jake.

"So what do we do?" Jake asked, turning to look at the long train of men and equipment following behind.

Night Wolf guessed the question. "Andres and I have found a place where you will be on the river but far away from Sotero's camp. You can stay there, but you will need to set guards. Your people will be waiting there," he said to Abby, then he and Andres rode away.

9

As camp was being set up on a grassy meadow near the river, Abby was greeted by her Kumeyaay family, what was left of them after small pox had nearly decimated their village. Her brother Weatuk was now a grown man and one of the council. Following the death of their head elder Wahss, Chico had stepped into his place as their leader.

There were a few new babies, and in spite of them being forced to give up their original village to Sotero, they were thriving. The many oak trees helped provide food, they grew a few crops, and raised chickens as well as a small herd of sheep.

Abby drew Weatuk aside. "How are things going with Sotero here?"

Weatuk scowled. "We stay away from him, and have to guard our women. They've already taken one against her will and refuse to return her. Sotero married her to one of his men. They claim the best land, which was our village. You were here when it was built with the help of so many neighbors."

"They forced you to leave?"

"We had no choice. We moved as far from them as we could, among the rocks. But we do have some areas where we grow corn and beans."

"And you still have the oaks?"

"Yes, many oaks, or our children would go hungry."

"Do you still buy food from the store?"

"Yes, but carefully. Harkness refuses to use your money for Sotero and this has made him angry. Watch out for him."

Abby could feel his frustration.

"Can you make him leave your property?" Weatuk asked.

"I will talk to him, but Night Wolf says he will not leave peacefully."

"If not, your men have guns."

"They aren't soldiers or lawmen. These are surveyors, a peaceful group setting boundaries for the reservations," Abby said, seeing her people making the surveyors welcome, and bringing gifts of food and making them elderberry tea.

Jake and his group seemed awkward with the

unfamiliar situation, but were friendly.

Bertram rode up to her, leading her horse, saddled and ready to ride. Behind was a group of mules to carry supplies from the store.

"We're going for supplies. Most of ours were stolen," he told Weatuk. "Be on the lookout for four or five white men with mules."

"We will watch," Weatuk said.

Abby mounted her horse and led the way toward the Cuyamaca store. Several well-armed men rode with them. As they passed by Sotero's village, Abby didn't see him, but she felt his eyes on her. Her medicine senses told her he was a very dangerous man, and there would be trouble.

Sidney Harkness was scowling as he stepped out on the front porch of his store. He didn't look happy to see Bertram and the mules, which indicated the need for a lot of supplies.

"Howdy, Miz Butterfield," he greeted Abby friendly enough as she stepped down from her horse. "I was told you'd be a'comin."

"Is something wrong, Mr. Harkness?"

Bertram dismounted and came up on the porch beside her. She introduced the two men.

"You don't look happy to see us," Bertram said as they shook hands.

"I was told you were coming and needing lots of supplies. That you've had some stolen," Harkness said.

"That's right. We're hoping you can help us out," Bertram said with a frown at the storekeeper's obvious reluctance.

"It's not the supplies that are the problem," Harkness said. "The problem is my having to bill the government. I'm still waiting on payment for supplies I sold to a company of soldiers six months ago. I need money to replace what you take, and don't have that much on hand. A lot of the locals barter with me rather than pay cash."

A frown marred Bertram's weathered face as he grasped the problem and scratched his bearded chin. "And I'd have to send to San Diego for cash...which will take over a week...if the Surveyor's Office even has it available."

For a moment there was silence as the three of them considered the dilemma. Finally Abby broke the silence. "Mr. Harkness, how much money do you have in my account?"

"Well, maybe enough to outfit you for a few days."

"Do you have anyone you can send to my ranch who you would trust with the money?"

For a moment Harkness looked thoughtful.

"Well, Brian Carter is due here today. We call him our Pony Express, but he's our Mail Express, he delivers mail on horseback all over these mountains. Only, rarely does that includes money."

"Yes, I know Brian," Abby said, "He delivers mail to the ranch. If I write a letter to my son Danny, Brian can go there, collect the money and bring it to you. Then when the government pays you, you can repay me."

Harkness was suddenly smiling. "Yes, ma'am, that would work just fine," He looked to Bertram who was also smiling with relief. "Let's get your supplies."

While the supplies were being selected and loaded onto the mules, Abby sat in Harkness's office and wrote a letter to Danny. He would know where the cash was hidden, and how to secure it into an innocent looking pouch for transportation.

Brian Carter, the mail delivery person for the back country, was a young man in his thirties, known for his fast horse, a quick draw with his six-shooter, and an equal quickness with a knife. The few robbers who had attempted to waylay him had not fared well, and since most of what he carried was only mail, not valuables, he was rarely a targeted by outlaws.

The Mail Express rider came in before the

loading of the mules was complete. Boyish looking, with long hair held back by a bandana tied across his forehead, and a scruffy beard, Brian was quick to grasp what was needed. He often delivered mail to Abby Butterfield's ranch, Eagles' Rest, and often timed his route so he could spend the night in their bunkhouse, and eat with her vaqueros.

"Glad to be of help, Miz Butterfield," he said with his boyish grin, looking down at the generous tip she had placed in his hand. "And glad for the extra money."

"In my letter I told Danny to be sure you get dinner and a place to spend the night. You can return with the money tomorrow."

"Yes, ma'am. I could use a hot meal and a bed in your bunkhouse."

With a wild whoop, Brian was off again at a gallop, headed for Eagles' Rest, a ride that would take him the rest of the day on the powerful quarter horse he called Rosie.

Harkness was more than happy to know he'd have his money the next day, and Abby returned to their camp with Bertram and the supply laden mules. This time, the supply tent was set up against giant boulders so no one could get at it from behind.

None of the workers complained about pulling guard duty, knowing how important it was that they not lose any more supplies. Often times, the promise of good food was one of the main inducements for men to volunteer for this type of wilderness duty.

That evening, the Kumeyaay invited the surveyors to their village in celebration of the return of their Eagle Woman.

The women wore their best dresses, some made of buckskin, some of the cotton given them by the former school teacher. From the teacher, they had been learning English, until Sotero forced her to leave.

Bertram and Jake left guards posted around their camp to discourage any further theft of their supplies.

Abby hadn't realized just how much she had missed the sound of the drums and the singing of the ancient songs. It brought back memories of her husband James Cassidy, and how he had come to her village looking for a wife, and had been shocked to find a young white woman living there. Further surprised when she reluctantly agreed to marry him. To fulfil her destiny, Abby knew she must return to the white world. Her visions had told her some of what lay ahead.

The memories of her deceased husband made her miss John Jay all the more. She remembered the night they met, when one of the husbands from a wagon train, after learning of her Indian background, tried to buy her favors with a few beads.

Her sharp blade set him straight, but she was taken by surprise when a handsome stranger stepped from the shadows laughing at how smoothly she had handled the situation. Abby often thought she fell in love with him right then, though many years passed before they could be together.

Now, watching the surveyors dancing in the circle around the fire, she couldn't help but smile at her memories, and of their acceptance of the Indian ways.

One of the women came for her, leading her into the women's circle, where she felt she belonged.

10

For the next few days, Abby was able to sleep in her people's village, staying in the ewa of the widows or women without family.

She became friends with a middle-aged woman who had taken the Spanish name Elena. Because the woman knew some of the medicine ways, they had much in common.

"We had a white teacher who came here," Elena told her. "Before Sotero and his people came. She was teaching our children, and anyone else who wanted to learn."

"She doesn't come now?" Abby asked, as they sat on a large boulder grinding acorns into a fine mash.

Other women around them were at similar rocks, doing the same preparation of the acorns to make them edible.

Elena scowled. "Sotero doesn't want us to learn

the white man's ways. He wants to be the head man who tells all of us what to do. Told her not to come back."

"Does she go to other villages?" Abby asked, realizing just how much of a danger Sotero and his huge ego could be to her people.

"Yes, and they are receptive. The people know they must speak as the white man does, learn about the laws so we can save our sacred places. These reservations you are here to mark are part of what we must understand…so that more men like Sotero can't come and push us off our land… your land." Elena looked very concerned. "How can you make him go? He will not go peacefully, or if he does, he will just take another village with his many hot blooded braves."

"I'm afraid it will take soldiers to move them," Abby said, stabbing her oval rock into the hole worn into the large boulder. It took centuries of such grinding of acorns to create such a hole. She wore a loose dress like the other women.

Hearing someone approaching, she looked up to see one of the older women from Sotero's camp, Red Bird. Sotero would not allow his people to take Spanish or Anglo names.

"Eagle Woman," she said dropping to her

knees before her, looking distressed. "I need your help. My sister, Little Deer, is very ill. Sotero only chants and waves burning sage over her. Still she coughs and her breathing is loud. I fear she will be with our ancestors before another night passes."

Abby looked from her to Elena. "I must go there. But first I need my medicine bag." As they walked to Sotero's camp Abby gathered leaves that would ease Little Deer's breathing.

Red Bird led her to the ewa where her sister lay, coughing, her breathing labored. Sotero was chanting and waving sage over her, but when he saw Abby, his face turned red with anger.

"We do not need you!" he raged. "I am medicine man. I will cure her."

"Look at her!" Abby said pointing to the sick woman. "You are not helping. I know the medicine ways. I can help her."

"You leave," he snarled. "You not touch her! I cure!"

It was all Abby could do not to physically attack the man. He was not helping the woman and Abby knew she would probably not survive the night. With no choice but to leave, Abby drew Red Bird aside. "We must make a medicine tea."

Red Bird helped heat the water to steep the

herbs Abby had gathered.

"Take this to your sister. Tell Sotero she must have nourishment, and you have brought her some tea. Tell him I left, that his medicine is strong, that you believe in him."

Even though Red Deer scowled at the thought of saying such things to Sotero, she would do anything to save her sister's life, which was now in her hands.

"Later, during the night, you will take her more. She must drink it all. She has something the white man calls pneumonia. Not everyone survives it, but with the tea, at least she will have a chance."

The ruse worked. When Red Bird took the tea to her sister, Sotero saw no harm in the nourishment. The coughing was obviously worse, but as Red Bird sat with her sister, she noticed a gradual easing of her breathing.

"You are helping, great warrior," Red Bird said, trying to keep a straight face.

Sotero's scowl of suspicion changed to a swelling of his chest.

"You are a great medicine man," she forced herself to say. She knew it was necessary if she was to save her sister's life.

Later in the night, Abby prepared more of the medicine tea, and when Red Bird entered her sister's ewa, Sotero was asleep on his robes and didn't awaken as she gave her sister more tea.

Already Little Deer's breathing had eased. Red Bird also brought her broth for nourishment. When she left the ewa, her sister had fallen into a peaceful sleep. She reported to Abby, who was then able to return to her own camp. Sotero would be full of himself when Little Deer recovered, but it was the only way they could save her life.

The following morning Abby was mounted and on her way back to the surveyor's camp when Night Wolf and Andres were suddenly next to her. More trouble, she thought, seeing Night Wolf's tight expression.

"What's happening?" she asked, looked from Andres to Night Wolf.

"More trouble, maybe," Night Wolf said. "But I thought your people should know. Along the big river there has been a horse thief troubling my people and the white soldiers. He is called Yellow Sky. He has been seen at several ranchos and even villages near here. Your people need to be aware and guard your horses. We have others spreading the word."

Abby scowled at the news. "What else can go wrong? Supplies stolen. Now we have to guard our horses too. Thank you, Night Wolf, for the warning."

With that the two men turned away and disappeared into the trees.

When Abby reached the surveyor's camp, she told Bertram, who was just clearing away the breakfast plates and coffee cups. He, too, scowled at the news. "I'll alert the men here, and Jake when he gets back. We don't have mounts to spare. Any luck getting that Sotero guy to leave your land?"

Abby shook her head. "He says that it is Indian land and he's staying. It's going to take the army to remove him."

"You going to ask them to?"

"Yes, I have to. They've pushed my people back into the rocks. There are still small areas of land where they can grow a few crops, and they're near water, but it is not as good as what Sotero has taken.

That day Mail Express rider Brian Carter had returned from Abby's ranch with the money for Harkness's supplies. Enough supplies had been purchased so that when the survey party rode out to the next day's location, they took plenty of food for their mid-day meal.

When Brian left the Cuyamaca Store, he was

on his way to the Carrillo Rancho, and to a few other settlers along his mail route.

At lunch time, he stopped at a favorite shady spot along the San Luis Rey River. This was also a nice break for Rosie as he unsaddled her to let her graze on the lush grass. He knew she wouldn't wander off, and she always liked to have a good roll, scratching her back from the constant weight of the saddle.

Mail was light this day, and Brian was dozing in the shade of an oak tree, in no hurry to leave. He was jarred awake by Rosie's snort of alarm. He looked up in time to see a large Indian, mounted on a strong looking appaloosa, who had surprised Rosie with a rope around her neck.

Leaping to his feet, Brian drew his gun but couldn't fire because Rosie was bucking and thrashing to get free. The rope tightened about her neck choking her until she was forced to follow.

"Rosie! Rosie! Let her go you bastard!"

Brian could hear the Indian's laughter at his helplessness, and how he relished taking possession of this beautiful mare.

Realizing the futility of fighting the rope, Rosie suddenly changed her tactics and charged her captor's appaloosa. First she bit the horse on his haunch, dodging his flashing hooves as he kicked at her with an angry snort. The Indian was suddenly fighting to control his own horse. Rosie's next bite was on the thigh of the Indian, who lost his grip on the rope as he yelled at Rosie, kicking to fight her off.

With one last bite on the appaloosa's withers, Rosie spun around, leaving the Indian struggling to control his bucking mount, and galloped toward Brian, the rope dragging behind her.

Brian could only fire over the Indian's head to keep him moving as he disappeared into the thick brush along the river.

Holstering his gun, Brian threw his arms around his thoroughly aroused mare, who snorted and stamped in triumph. He removed the rope from around her neck, as Rosie rubbed her head against him, muttering softly.

"Guess you surprised him, love. Good girl! This is a nice rope, I think I'll keep it."

Brian looped the rope and tied it to his saddle, and, too keyed up by the excitement to rest any more, he saddled and bridled Rosie and they were off on their route. They couldn't help but watch out for any further sign of the Indian, and spread the word to everyone they met.

The story of Brian's encounter with the Indian presumed to be the horse thief Yellow Sky quickly spread throughout the area, and Rosie became a legend.

Whenever Yellow Sky encountered other Indians, or tried to find respite in a local village, the story of his encounter with the Mail Express rider preceded him and he found he was a laughing stock. He soon disappeared from the area and was never seen there again.

11

Danny stepped out onto the back steps of the house into the crisp, cool, morning air, holding a cup of coffee to warm his hands. He was tall for a sixteen year old, and had filled out nicely since being adopted by the Butterfields. His blue eyes scanned the mountains west of the ranch, knowing the heavy layer of clouds above them would eventually bring rain. Maybe two days from now.

Before then, they needed to finish mowing the hay and picking the extensive apple crop.

The ranch foreman said he had hired two temporary workers the previous day, which would help them beat the storm. It wasn't unusual to find drifters or temporary workers, staying when needed, then drifting on with a few dollars in their pockets.

Mandy stepped outside beside him, a warm shawl wrapped around her shoulders. She, too, looked at the distant clouds and realized any work on the ranch needed to be stepped up.

"Delfina and I will bring the children out after breakfast and gather the ripe vegetables from the garden," she told him. "By tomorrow we can start canning."

Danny nodded his approval. "Good. I'm going to be busy out in the fields and feeding the stock."

"Breakfast is almost ready, why don't you get washed up."

Mandy went inside, and after another moment of surveying the quiet of the ranch, Danny followed.

In the bunkhouse there was a crude kitchen where one of the vaqueros could also fix breakfast for the workers. In addition to Pete, the foreman, there were four full time vaqueros.

Later, Danny rode out to the fields to watch the men cutting the rich, ripe hay. He loved the fresh scent of it. And it looked like they would be able to clear the fields before the storm reached them. In spite of his young age, the workers called him Jefe, meaning Chief, and he had their respect.

Seeing that the haying was under control, he rode to the apple orchard where three men were picking fruit. One was a regular ranch hand, Armando, the others the two drifters Pete had hired. They weren't yet aware of his presence, and as Danny watched them, he frowned. One of the men looked familiar, like maybe he'd seen him when he'd lived on the streets in Los Angeles.

Their work was slow, as if they had no real interest in what they were doing. One of them came down from his ladder with a bucket only half full of apples and dumped them, with unnecessary roughness, into a big box. Apples needed to be handled carefully or they would bruise. The man then moved a short distance away to relieve himself. As Danny turned away, he was still trying to recall where he'd seen the one man before. When he glanced back, he saw the drifter who was still on a ladder was watching him, but looked away quickly, furtively.

"Trouble," Danny muttered to himself. He rode back to the field to find the foreman, or head vaquero, Pete. He dismounted where Pete was using a pitchfork to load freshly mowed hay onto a wagon.

"Know anything about those two new men?" Danny asked.

Pete was past middle age but had worked for the

former owner for a number of years. His knowledge had been a big help to the inexperienced Butterfields when they first bought the ranch.

"Only that their names are Charlie and Bart. Said they've worked a few places around Temecula, but had a hankering to explore the back country," he said, pushing his hat back and mopping his forehead with his handkerchief. "They heard about this place and thought they'd give us a try, before they move on to the Warner area." Pete saw Danny's frown. "A problem?" he asked.

"I don't know…but something don't feel right. Keep an eye on them. I'll be doing the same."

Danny rode back to the barn to feed the horses and milk the cows. A small herd of sheep was grazing the field they had mowed the previous day, eating anything that was missed.

It was a normal day at the ranch. When the stock was fed, Danny mounted his horse and waved to Mandy and Delfina in the garden where they were picking carrots, zucchini, tomatoes and any other ripe vegetables. Little Jay was helping by taking full baskets to dump into a lug box. Ellie was sleeping on a blanket in the sun nearby where they could watch over her.

All morning Danny had been bothered by the

two drifters, so he rode back to the orchard. When he checked their amount of apples, their boxes showed far fewer than the regular ranch hand.

He caught a glimpse of one of them on the ground staring up at the sky, then heard a gunshot.

A large female golden eagle whirled past him at tree top level, and Danny saw the man taking aim again. Spurring his horse, Danny dove from his back, grabbed the man's gun arm and carried him to the ground. The gun went off harmlessly.

"What do you think you're doing?" Danny demanded, straddling the man.

"I'm shootin' that big bird!" he said angrily.

"That big bird is a golden eagle. We don't shoot them!" He took the man's six shooter from his hand, stood up and emptied the rest of the bullets onto the dirt. "Do you know what the name of this ranch is?" Danny demanded.

The man shrugged. "Didn't ask."

"It's called Eagles' Rest, and around here those birds are part of the ranch. They eat the rats and squirrels that eat our fruit and the rabbits who get into the garden."

"Oh," was all he could say.

"Now get back to work," Danny ordered. "You two are way behind Armando."

"You ain't the boss," Bart complained.

"When my parents are away, I am the boss. And if you don't like that you can collect your pay right now!" He gave a derisive look at their meager pickings. "Which won't be much."

Though he was grumbling, Bart took back the gun Danny was holding out to him and turned back to his bucket and ladder. Danny went back to his horse, and as he mounted he was aware of Charlie watching him from atop his ladder, but again turned away quickly. If it weren't for the approaching storm, and his need to complete the harvest, he would have sent both men packing.

Later that afternoon, while Danny was out in the fields, Mandy was in the kitchen preparing vegetables for the evening mutton stew. A sound behind her startled her and she turned to find a stranger had come silently in the back door and was looking everything over with a quick assessment.

"What are you doing in here?" she demanded.

Charlie's gaze came back to her, trying to look sheepish. "No harm, ma'am," he muttered. "I was hopin' I could get some of that good lemonade we had last night."

Mandy knew it for the lie it was and was glad she had a sharp knife in her hand. Her eyes flashed with fire. "You don't ever come in this house without knocking. If you want lemonade you go see Rico at the bunkhouse!"

"Oh," he tried to look chagrined. "I didn't know," and he went out.

Mandy stared after him for a long time, bothered by the incident. The man had been too interested in what he saw in the house, especially the number of heirlooms scattered about.

That night at dinner, she told Danny about the incident. "He just walked in?" Danny asked, startled.

"Yes. No knock. I never heard him until I turned and saw him. Said he came for some lemonade, but I know that ain't true. He was lookin' everything over real good."

"I knew those two were going to be trouble," he doubled his fists on either side of his plate, asking himself what John Jay would do. "Tomorrow I'll tell Pete they're done at the end of the day, to come to the house the next morning to collect their pay before they ride out."

The morning after, Danny knew better than to have the strong box with any money in sight. He had the money ready for the two when they came up to the house. Though they tried to act like it was just time to ride on, their furtive looks took in the alcove which served as the ranch office, and everything they could see.

Danny ushered them to the back door where their saddled horses waited. "Thanks for the help," Danny said as if this were a normal termination.

The two men merely acknowledged with a wave of their hand and rode out. Danny didn't move from the doorway as he watched them head out on the trail toward Warner Springs.

Mandy came up beside him. "Good riddance."

"I don't think we've seen the last of them." Danny looked troubled. "They were too nosy. Keep a rifle handy for the next few days." Then he went off to talk to Pete and the others.

Workers rarely carried weapons, but now they either wore a six-shooter or had a rifle handy. And their gazes frequently scanned the surrounding area.

At the end of the day, Pete met with Danny in the barn as they unsaddled their horses and spent time currying and feeding them.

"You don't think they're gone, do you?" Pete asked.

Danny shook his head. "They were too interested in the house, and the coin I paid them. Probably thinking there's more where that came from."

When they finished grooming their horses,

they turned them into stalls with fresh hay for food and bedding.

"We need to post guards on the stock and the house, but I doubt they'll come tonight," Danny said, sounding far more mature then his sixteen years. "They'll give us time to forget them, and let our guard down."

"But we won't take any chances," Pete agreed.

"No, you make up a schedule of guards, and I'll take my turn too. Four hour shifts."

In the house, Danny alerted Mandy and Delfina to the possible danger. Both women knew how to handle a rifle, and kept theirs close. Then he checked all the windows to be certain they were locked, something they rarely did, as well as locking the front and back doors for the night.

"We'll be on guard outside," he assured them.

As expected, there was no sighting of the two drifters the first night. The next morning, as Danny looked toward the approaching storm, he saw the two eagles circling high over the hillside forest of oak trees. He knew their nest was somewhere in a side canyon farther into the hills. It was also a good place to camp unseen. He suspected that was where the drifters would be.

Though there was less danger during the day,

with so many men around, Pete still arranged a work schedule that kept several men around the ranch house at all times. They tried not to make it obvious they were on their guard.

A group of riders was still some distance away when they were spotted, and Danny came outside immediately to watch their approach. Even from a distance he could see one was wearing a badge. Danny recognized Marshall Barker, having seen him before in Los Angeles, and his previous visit here to the ranch. Four deputies rode with him, and after greeting and handshakes, Danny invited them to water their horses, and Mandy graciously offered to make them sandwiches.

"That would be much appreciated, ma'am," the Marshall said. "We've been on the trail for days, searching for two men who robbed the Jenkin's ranch last week."

Danny and the Marshall sat at the kitchen table to eat, while his men were content to eat outside in the shade of the porch.

"Who are they?" Danny asked as they bit into their roast beef sandwiches, served with some of Mandy's potato salad.

"Charlie Black and Bart Sampson. A couple of no accounts. They used to hang around Los Angeles.

We think they're the ones who broke into a couple of stores there at night. When I went looking to question them I was told they'd left town."

"I thought I remembered Charlie from Los Angeles," Danny said. "He always had his nose in places it didn't belong."

"Now it looks like they hire on as temporary workers while they check the place out, then make their move at night."

Danny lowered his sandwich and looked steadily at the Marshall. "You want to help set a trap for them?"

"A trap. How?" he sounded interested.

"They worked here until the day before yesterday. I didn't trust them, and I'm thinking they'll be back tonight."

"That sounds like their usual method. You got a plan worked out?"

"Yes, we posted guards last night, hidden. But I wouldn't expect them until tonight, when we'd supposedly think they'd moved on."

The Marshall nodded. "You think they're watching?"

"They could be...could know you're here. I suggest you and your men ride out like you're going on your way. I'll send Rico with you to show you how to get back to the rear of the barn un-seen," Danny said. "You can stay there until dark, then we'll show you where to stand guard where you won't be seen."

"Sounds like a damn good plan. I really want to nail those two galoots, or they'll just keep robbin' folks."

"I'm really glad you showed up, Marshall. I wasn't sure what we'd do if they came, shoot 'em or tie 'em up."

"Sometimes they don't give you a choice," the Marshall said. "You do what you have to. Only to-night, it will be me and my men setting the trap."

When darkness came, the Marshall and one of his men were sneaked into the house, hiding in the parlor and kitchen. The other three were shown hiding spots where they could watch the house. The vaqueros would be guarding the stock.

Danny purposely unlocked a window in the main dining room. He suspected the men would want to search the office alcove for a strong box. From there, they'd take anything they thought they could sell. Armed with a rifle and a six shooter, Danny stood in the shadows where he could see the window, and, across the yard to the barn.

It was after midnight when Danny saw movement

in the shadows beside the barn. "Here they come," he whispered.

The two lawmen stood in silence as the two drifters came to the house and began trying doors and windows until they found the one Danny had left unlocked. Very quietly they eased the window open and climbed inside, each one carrying a large flour sack.

Danny crouched in the shadows as the Marshall had instructed him. And, as expected, the men went straight to the office alcove and began opening drawers, seeking out any possible hiding spot for a strong box.

At the Marshall's signal, his deputy struck a match and lit a lamp.

"Can we help you boys?" the Marshall asked.

Charlie turned toward the voice, his right hand reaching for his gun. Marshall Barker already had his gun in his hand and fired, the bullet piercing Charlie's right shoulder.

"Don't shoot! Don't shoot!" Bart yelled, raising his hands high in the air.

Danny came into the room, rifle in hand and picked up the gun Charlie had dropped. The deputy took the gun from Bart's holster.

Charlie was cussing a blue streak as he clutched

his wounded arm trying to stop the flow of blood. "How'd you know?" he demanded.

"We've followed you long enough to know your tricks," the Marshall told him.

"But we saw you ride out," Bart whined. "You left."

"No," Danny told him. "We suspected you were watching, so they rode out and snuck back."

Charlie cussed again.

More lamps were lit as Mandy came from the bedrooms, where Delfina was soothing the frightened children awakened by the shot. "The gun shot woke us," she said seeing the situation was under control.

"I'm bleeding bad!" Charlie whined.

Seeing Mandy was carrying a medicine bag, the Marshall motioned Charlie to sit the kitchen table, pulling out a chair for him. "Sit! And let the lady patch you up. Just be thankful you're still breathing. I could have aimed a bit lower."

Danny unlocked the back door to let the other deputies in. They handcuffed Bart and took him outside while the Marshall took his knife and cut Charlie's shirt to expose the wound. Luckily, the bullet had gone clean through his shoulder.

Setting his rifle down, Danny washed his hands and helped Mandy pack the two wounds with herbs to stop any infection, then tore strips of a sheet to bind it tightly to stop the bleeding.

"We'll head back to Los Angeles in the morning," the Marshall said. "The doctor there can check him out again, but it looks like you've done a good job."

"My ma is a medicine woman," Danny said proudly. "We've learned just from watching her."

"You used to be in Los Angeles," Charlie grumbled. "In the streets. Stealing food."

Danny grinned. "Naw, I never had to steal. Some places left food out for me or else I rummaged through their trash. But I never stole."

"There are probably a few open beds in the bunkhouse," Mandy told the Marshall, "And we could make up a bed in the parlor."

"We may use the bunkhouse," the Marshall said, pulling Charlie to his feet and slapping his dropped hat on his head. "But mostly we'll use the barn. We brought our own bedrolls, and I imagine Charlie and Bart have horses close by ready to ride."

Once they'd gone out, Danny looked at Mandy who was still wearing her day dress. "Good job, medicine woman," he said with a smile.

"Abby is a good teacher. We both learned from

her." She cleaned up the bloody rags, while Danny went to lock the window, though he was certain there wouldn't be any more trouble tonight.

"I don't know about you," Mandy said. "But I'm too keyed up to sleep. Would you like some hot chocolate?"

"That sounds mighty good."

"You done good," Mandy told him as she started the preparations. "Abby and John Jay will be mighty proud of you."

"They trusted me to run this ranch while they're gone. Darned if I'll let anything happen to it."

12

Whenthe time came to establish the boundaries for the Kupa Village at Warner Hot Springs, Abby rode along to see how they were faring.

More and more, as she visited villages, she saw the Indian ewa dwellings were giving way to larger wooden or adobe homes.

At the Hot Springs, Abby was surprised to see adobe buildings and a thriving business. People came from as far away as Los Angeles and San Diego to soak in the hot waters, and often stayed for days. There were several other villages set far back in the rugged hill country but which were of no interest to the white settlers. However, the survey and the formal granting of reservations by Washington would ensure their right to the land called Los Coyotes.

In some areas, Newton Booth, the Governor of California, had granted land to settlers without checking with the Indian Agency, creating a legal battle that would take many years to untangle. The Governor said one thing, the President and Congress decreed something else. Both the settlers and the Indian families were left without clear titles and much confusion.

School teachers were engaged for some of the larger villages to teach the children, and often the grownups too. And Abby noticed more and more Indians were taking Anglo or Spanish names.

With Night Wolf and Andres going ahead to contact the various villages, there was an acceptance of the white men with the strange devices. And they continued to spread the story of the mail rider's encounter with the horse thief Yellow Sky. The villagers found it hilarious and Yellow Sky dared not show his face anywhere in the mountains.

Abby sat on a log near the fire that evening in their camp. She'd been with the surveyors for over a month and was very much missing her family. Especially since she was now so close to Eagles' Rest. As she stood up to return her empty plate to Bertram's cleanup crew, she spotted a lone horseman barely visible in the lengthening twilight.

Suddenly her tin plate went flying as she gave a whoop of joy, running and flinging herself into her husband's open arms. They were laughing, talking over each other as John Jay hauled her up in front of him, kissing her as if he'd never get enough.

"Brian told me where to find you," he said hugging her close. "I grabbed a fresh horse and came straight here. And I'm starving."

Bertram and his crew were pleased to meet John Jay, had plenty of food left, and were eager to hear stories from Washington.

Sadly, John Butterfield Senior had died peacefully in his sleep. John Jay's mother, heart-broken though she was, had been prepared for that inevitable end. John Jay stayed long enough to settle his father's affairs and make certain his mother was well provided for, his brothers there to help ease the pain. They would be close by when John Jay returned to his family in California by any means he could find: trains, stage coaches and horseback.

Along the way he'd written to Governor Booth, as well as the Indian Commissioner in San Diego, letting them know what was happening in Congress. The many treaties formulated by the California Indian Agents in the past remained missing, and no amount of prodding from him or the

President could locate them.

Abby and John Jay could hardly keep their hands off each other. When they could finally make their escape, they went to a quiet place along the Sweetwater River that ran through her property. Shedding their clothes they dove into a large pool, both of them needing to be free of days and days of trail dust. Frolicking in the water, they played like children, splashed each other, then stopping now and then to hug and kiss, then splash some more. Finally they tumbled out onto the lush grass and made love, at first frantically, then slowly and sweetly.

"I missed you so damn much," he murmured as they lay, exhausted. "I could barely kiss the kids hello, meet your cousin Mandy, and then jump on a fresh horse. I can't believe how much Danny has grown. He'll be a man soon. And, it's a good thing Brian was there. He told me where to find you." He held her away from him and gave her a wry look. "Indian Agent? You? I couldn't believe that. Yet, it makes perfect sense. The Indians trust you."

"It's been a long, difficult task, but the Indians are cooperating. They've been promised so much, and given so little. I wouldn't have blamed them if they hadn't accepted us."

"And, even when the survey is complete, there

aren't any guarantees that squatters won't move in before President Grant receives all this survey information and can act on it." John Jay said. "When I wrote to Governor Booth, I passed along the President's message that he not grant any more land in this area until the reservation situation is finalized."

"We're having a problem right here at Green Valley, and the squatters aren't white, they're Indian."

Abby told him about Sotero pushing her people out of their homes and into the back country.

"Sounds like big trouble," John Jay said, frowning.

"It's going to take the army to force him out, and I dread taking that step, but one of Sotero's men took a young girl from the Kumeyaay camp as his wife. She had no say in the matter." Abby was silent for a moment, a deep frown marring her forehead. "My people have to guard their women. They often see Sotero's braves stalking their camp, and they're afraid. Our men go armed with knives and bows constantly. Guns if they have them. Something they've never had to do before.

"Have you informed the Captain at Camp Wright?"

"Not yet, but now that you're here, a letter from

you will carry a lot more weight."

"We'll also want letters from Jake Wilcox, and Sidney Harkness at Cuyamaca."

"Good idea. Captain Oatman won't be able to ignore that, and Sotero won't back down unless he's forced to."

"We'll do that tomorrow. But now," he pulled her closer, his hands stroking her naked bottom. "I have something else in mind."

"Oh?" she said teasingly. "And what would that be?"

"I'm going to make mad, passionate love to my wife."

"Lucky woman," she breathed as his lips took hers.

It was a long time before they came up for air, and took another plunge into the river. They clung together for a long time before finally dressing and creeping into the sleeping camp to Abby's tent.

The two men standing guard were grinning as they turned away, pretending not to see their disheveled condition.

The next day, John Jay conferred with Head Surveyor Jake Wilcox who agreed to write a letter to the army, too. He'd just become aware that Sotero and his men were spreading false rumors about the surveyors and what their mission was regarding the land. Obviously they wanted the white men and Abby gone.

Fortunately Night Wolf and Andres were also there to counteract the lies. And it was also fortunate that in most villages, Sotero's men were mistrusted for their inflammatory words urging the villages to fight the white surveyors.

The letter to Camp Wright took on a new urgency. Harkness at the Cuyamaca store added his letter to the ones from John Jay and Jake.

When Brian Carter showed up with the mail, John Jay impressed on him the importance of the letters to Camp Wright, which lay west of Warner Hot Springs. It was a long ride, not Brian's usual route, but he realized the situation here was becoming dire, and soon he and Rosie were off in a cloud of dust.

Sotero must have suspected something was up because two Indians were soon on Brian's trail. Ever alert in this back country, even Rosie knew they were being stalked. The chase began. Rosie's long legs and grain-fed muscles carried her and Brian far faster than the grass fed Indian ponies, and she soon outdistanced them.

Brian also knew this country like the back of his

hand, and soon lost their pursuers. But from then on, he and Rosie were on high alert. Not risking a fire when they stopped for the night, he wiped Rosie's hot body down with bunches of grass. Her hearing was far better than his, and she would warn him if by some chance their pursuers hadn't given up. Only when he'd cared for her did Brian prepare his own dry meal, the two of them staying hidden among a scattering of giant boulders.

Two of the survey crew galloped up to John Jay at the Cuyamaca store.

"We saw two Injuns chasing Brian, but we were too far away to help."

John Jay and two more surveyors sprang into their saddles and tore off at a gallop the way the surveyors pointed. They'd only gone a few miles when they reined in sharply. In the valley below, two Indians on obviously exhausted horses were headed back toward Green Valley. With a whoop of laughter, John Jay turned back, the two surveyor's laughter joining his. The mail would reach Camp Wright safely, and now they needed to make plans for the coming military presence.

Sotero stormed angrily among a gathering of his

warriors. "You let him go!" he blasted the two riders.

"His horse was too fast. We were never close enough to use a rifle," one of the pursuers said, standing tall before Sotero's withering glare. "He will bring soldiers."

That statement brought a lot of talk among the warriors. "We have families here," one said. "The soldiers will force us out. I go to my woman's village."

Several others agreed.

"We will not be here when soldiers come," another said.

"Cowards!" Sotero blasted them. "We must stay and fight!"

But his words fell on deaf ears and soon preparations were being made by most of the families to move away from this suddenly dangerous location…until, hours later, only Sotero and a few warriors were left standing alone in a deserted village.

The medicine man was furious as he and his men reluctantly gathered up their weapons and personal gear. As they left the area, they were aware of Abby, John Jay and Jake watching.

"Eagle Woman will pay for this," he vowed, knowing she considered this to be her land. Being driven out by a mere woman was humiliating.

Abby watched the departing warriors with a feeling of relief. One of the survey crew, familiar with the area, headed for Camp Wright with the news that the military was no longer needed.

Along the way he met up with Brian on his way back with the news that the soldiers were currently out on another situation in the San Bernardino Mountains and would not be available for over a week.

The rider was relieved to hear the news, but continued on to Camp Wright, while Brian carried the news to Harkness at the store, then to Abby at the surveyors' camp.

13

Abby stepped out of her tent in the morning, feeling content for the first time in weeks after snuggling next to John Jay all night. He was still sleeping, recovering from the long, hard cross country trek. As she poured herself a cup of coffee at the mess table, she saw that Jake had all of his plats spread out on the ground nearby, with rocks to hold the corners down. He had them arranged in the position of the areas he was surveying. And was muttering to himself.

"Jake, good morning," she greeted him. "Something wrong?"

"Oh yeah, Mrs. Abby." That was the name they'd settled on when she asked him to call her Abby instead of Mrs. Butterfield. "Everything is wrong. And this survey isn't going as it should. In places that should be potential reservation land, I'm finding squatters. Some even know it's supposed to be Indian land, but say it's too good for 'heathens'."

"I was afraid of that."

"Plus, they can go into Los Angeles and find some Indian that's been arrested for drunkenness, pay his bail and make him work for them to pay it off. They're making the Indian little more than a slave."

"This whole system in California seems geared for the extermination of Indians," Abby's sad look spoke volumes.

"Even more disturbing," Jake went on. "Some squatters even know it's supposed to be Indian reservation and are hoping the government will pay them off to get them to move."

For a time they were silent, contemplating the areas on the plats where white squatters had built a home, chopping down trees the Indians relied on for food, planting crops, and allowing sheep to graze on Indian land.

"What can we do?" Abby asked, almost to herself, saddened by what she was seeing.

Jake took a deep breath, a look of resolve transforming to anger. "We finish the survey and we let the Governor and the President know what's happening."

"They need to act now!" Abby added. "To stop this!"

"We just have a couple more sites to do yet. We'll be moving camp tomorrow. I want to finish this and file my reports as soon as possible."

Abby felt tears gathering in her eyes. "Jake, thank you for caring."

"How can you help but see what is happening to these first people. Everything from extermination to slavery."

"Which they dress up by calling it indenturing."

Jake began rolling up his plats. "Today I'll be going to the Laguna Mountain area. That'll take the entire day, traveling, surveying. Your Indian friends have told the village there that we're coming."

"Then I think I'll stay here today," Abby said. "There's a baby due at my People's village."

"We should be okay on our own," Jake said preparing his surveying equipment for the trek. At the far side of the camp, Abby could see Jake's helpers readying their mounts and the day's supplies "Your friend Night Wolf has done a good job of telling the People we're trying to help them keep their land."

John Jay came out of their tent, stretching lazily,

and giving his wife a sexy grin. "Good morning, Mrs. Butterfield, how was your night?"

"For some reason, I didn't get much sleep."

"Strange. Neither did I. But at least I got to sleep in." He looked at the cup she was holding. "Any more of that coffee around?"

"Yes, but you'd better hurry. The surveyors are on their way to their next village, and Bertram will be closing the kitchen."

John Jay got to the table just in time for a cup of very black coffee and the remains of the crew's breakfast. Abby joined him, taking her breakfast also. Not caring there wasn't much left. They were too satisfied from the night of loving to care.

Night Wolf and Andres sat on their horses hidden amongst the oak trees. They had come to contact a small village sitting along the stream flowing out of the mountains toward the old stagecoach road.

For hundreds of years the seasonal village here was peaceful and thriving. Now the two men saw no signs of it. All they saw along the stream were tents and men panning for gold. They'd been told white men were flocking to all the mountain streams in this area where gold had been discovered several years earlier. And when men searched for gold they often became crazy with gold fever. News had spread quickly to the Indian villages in the area, as one after the other fled from the miners. It was either flee or be wiped out.

From early years of Spanish occupation the Indians had long known how to search for the gold pebbles and flakes used to buy things. Always using only small amounts, they gave only vague stories of where it came from. They learned caution after what had happened to the tribes along the Sacramento River, where villages had been wiped out and Indians killed for resisting. In the end, the entire gold country was taken over by thousands of seekers with gold fever.

The two turned back, staying out of sight of the white men, and went to a village further downstream. But even before they reached it, they knew what they would find…a tent town, loud voices, men panning, arguing, and deer meat roasting over an open fire.

Discouraged, Night Wolf and Andres turned back toward Cuyamaca, intending to ask the owner of the store just how wide spread the gold was. Andres spoke better English, so Night Wolf would listen, knowing he had to learn the language if he intended to ask Mandy to be his wife.

They hadn't gone far when they saw two Indian families coming toward them with enough supplies to suggest they were moving. Night Wolf knew they were two Lakota Sioux brothers who had settled at the Santa Ysabel village after years on the renegade trail. Each family consisted of two horses and two mules packed with teepees and food. Each man had a wife and two children. One woman held an infant in a cradle, the other held a girl of two or three in front of her on the horse.

"Long Bow," Night Wolf greeted his old comrade from his renegade days. "You are moving from Santa Ysabel?"

The group took advantage of the encounter to stop in the shade of some tall cottonwood trees, to rest their animals and water them. There were snacks for the children.

"We go to a gathering of my father's clan at the Sun Dance, in a place the Whites call Montana," Long Bow told Night Wolf as he and Andres dismounted to share news.

"That is a long way to travel," Night Wolf remarked.

"True, but it is a tradition among my father's people, the Lakota. As a boy, our family attended every year, along with my brother here, Little Elk."

Night Wolf and Andres exchanged greetings with the brother.

"Now, we want our children to be part of this sacred ceremony. Many tribes from the Plains will be gathering."

For a time, Long Bow told about the ceremonies attended by most of the great Spiritual leaders of the Plains. Even though the various local clans held an annual fiesta, Night Wolf knew they were small gatherings compared to the Sun Dance which would cover a vast area of Rosebud Creek in Montana.

"Safe journey, my friend," Night Wolf said as he and Andres mounted their horses and again set out for Cuyamaca.

"I do not envy them that trip," Andres said, glancing back at the two families resting in the shade. "It is far."

"Nor I," Night Wolf said. "Though I have heard much about this great gathering."

"But, I also hear the soldiers are trying to force the Lakota and the Cheyenne onto reservations," Andres said, frowning at what that meant for the gathering. "This Sun Dance will bring all the tribes together in one place, many of them leaving reservations to attend. The soldiers will know this."

Night Wolf's frown said he had thought of that too. "I hope Long Bow and Little Elk do not regret choosing this year to take their families."

Harkness was sitting on the front steps of the store, watching the two Indians approach, sensing they were on a mission and not in need of supplies. He invited them to sit with him and offered tea as he often did on a lazy day like today.

Andres took a polite sip of the tea before getting to the point. "We visit Indian village," he said, pointing, not knowing a name for the area. "Now only white men after gold."

Harkness nodded. "They've been buying some of their supplies here, and have been finding small pockets of gold. Nothing big except in the valley just east of here, and it's brought would-be miners flocking to the area. They've started bringing in big equipment, which means a big find. Funny thing, a man was chasing his run away burro and found it as well as a shelf of gold."

"Do they know about river where Kumeyaay live?" Andres asked.

Night Wolf was following the conversation,

straining to understand.

"Well now…," Harkness drawled. "I told them a little fib. I told them the land belonged to John Jay Butterfield and his wife, and that Butterfield's father is a close friend of President Grant…which is mostly true."

"So they not go to Kumeyaay river?"

"It's called Sweetwater River. I told them that Butterfield owns all mineral rights." When Harkness saw the Indians frown at the strange words he elaborated. "That means if there's gold, it belongs to Butterfield, and anyone caught trying to pan his river will be arrested. Can't mine for gold if you're sitting in jail."

"Is good," Night Wolf said.

"We take message to medicine woman and the men marking the reservations," Andres said.

"Yes," Harkness agreed. "They need to know. There's always a chance some maverick miner will try his luck anyway."

The two men politely sipped the tea, well used to the Indian tradition of offering tea. To refuse was an insult to the hosts.

Then they mounted their horses and went to seek out the head surveyor, to tell him what they had found at the villages that would have been the next destination. Gone.

Fortunately most of the gold was found to the north east end of the survey area, and had little impact on the back country. Would-be miners crowded the streams and rivers, but because of earthquake faulting in that area, strikes became illusive. Only the one discovered by a run-away mule was a real success, and had become the largest producing mine in the area, named the Stonewall Mine.

Five days later, Abby and John Jay were back at Eagles' Rest Ranch catching up on chores let go during their absence. Though Danny and Mandy tried to keep up with things, along with the four vaqueros, there was still a lot to do. The supper dishes were done and Abby was putting the children to bed, while John Jay was in the alcove that served as his office catching up on correspondence. Mandy was busy folding the sheets and towels she'd brought in from the clothes lines, but feeling unaccountably lonesome. She hadn't seen Night Wolf in weeks and found herself having thoughts about being alone with him, touching his hard male body.

After what the brothers had done to her, she thought she'd never want a man to touch her that way again. Even though they hadn't been mean to her, she just wasn't allowed the option of saying no. Yet, when she thought about Night Wolf, her body tormented her with strange new sensations.

A familiar whistle sounded from outside, at the rear of the house. As if in answer to her thoughts, she looked out into the twilight to see the very man she was longing for. Without giving the laundry another thought, or even taking time to grab her shawl, she ran out the back door to the mounted warrior who scooped her up onto his horse in front of him and headed for the barn.

Abby had just come into the back porch to help Mandy when she saw them together. With a smile, she finished the chore of folding the laundry.

"I'm so glad to see you," Mandy said hugging him. "I've missed you."

"I've missed you," he said softly, holding her tightly against him. "I had to come."

"You...You're talking better English," she noticed.

"I've learned from the surveyors. If I want you to be my woman, I must learn to speak as you do."

Mandy hugged him again, snuggling into the warmth of his body, which was all the answer he needed.

Guiding his horse into the open door of the barn, he slid down then lifted Mandy down beside him. With lots of fresh hay piled in one corner, his pinto began to feed.

"I have made plans, if you agree," he said.

"Tell me later," she breathed as her lips sought his. They kissed as if they would never get enough. Somehow the front of her dress was open and his hot hands were stroking her breasts. Moments later, her undergarments were gone and his buckskin clothing formed a bed in the hay.

Mandy was on fire with feelings totally new to her. She couldn't have stopped them, didn't want to stop them as the warrior's body covered hers. This time there was no pain when his body joined hers. She welcomed him with a fiery passion.

She could only urge him on until she was swept to a glorious place she'd never been before, and Night Wolf's grunts of pleasure joined hers.

Slowly they came down from the heights. Awed by what they'd experienced.

"I want you for my wife," Night Wolf said when they were able to breathe normally again.

"Oh, yes," Mandy agreed.

Night Wolf moved to lay beside her, holding her close. "Wait to hear my plan, then say you agree or not."

Mandy tried to curb her impatience. It was

something that had to be discussed, though she didn't want anything to disturb this wonderful new feeling.

"To be my wife means to live as I live. I have never lived in a white man's house. Ewas, hogans, teepees, yes. But I have spoken with the elders at Green Valley. They build a house for us. They want me to teach the young men the ways of the warriors so they will know how to feed their families, and they hope you can teach the children."

Mandy's eyes lit up with excitement. "I've always wanted to be a teacher!"

"You would be far away from your family. It's a day's ride from here."

"Abby has told me about Green Valley, and the white families in the area as well as Indian. I know I will like it there."

"Is good," he said, and was kissing her again as they sealed their future life together.

Much later, when they came up for air, Mandy asked, "So will I be Mrs. Night Wolf?"

Night Wolf laughed at the thought. "No my beautiful wife-to-be, you will not be called Mrs. Night Wolf. I am taking a Spanish name, one given to me by one of the old ones at a village in the mountains. He has chosen the name Sostenes

Del Rio. You will be Mrs. Del Rio." He placed his hand over her slightly rounded belly. "And our son will also bear that name."

"What does it mean, Del Rio?"

"Of the river, because I come from the big river."

~

John Jay was in bed, propped up by pillows, watching Abby as she sat at her dressing table brushing out her long red hair, a slight smile on her lips. The two white wings at each of her temples seemed to glow in the flickering light of the kerosene lamp. He had never been prouder of having Abby for his wife, and proud of the work she had done in the back country with the survey party.

"What are you grinning about?" he asked, patting the bed next to him so she would come join him.

"I had to finish Mandy's laundry folding," she said, still smiling.

John Jay looked puzzled. "And?"

"And, along came Night Wolf, who scooped her up and carried her off to the barn…where I suspect they still are."

John Jay wasn't certain what to think about

that. He knew at one time Night Wolf had wanted Abby for his wife. "This is good?" he ventured.

"Yes, I think they fell in love. And, unless I miss my guess, Mandy won't be coming inside to her room tonight."

John Jay gave a soft laugh. "You obviously think that is a good thing."

"Mandy went through hell with those brothers. She deserves a good man who can love her in spite of the baby she carries. I doubt any white man would do that."

John Jay nodded, knowing she was right. He had come to respect Night Wolf after the Indian had saved his life and returned him to his wife, to a woman Night Wolf had loved but knew could never be his.

"I'm getting awfully cold over here," he said with a pretense of shivering. "I need someone to warm me."

Abby was laughing as she stood up from the bench, blew out the lamp and joined her husband under the covers. For someone who was claiming to be cold, he was shedding an awful lot of pajamas…and then, so was she.

14

The bed of freshly cut hay was soft and fragrant, and Night Wolf and Mandy didn't want to leave it. He got his robes from his horse, bedded him down for the night, and then they spent the rest of the night snuggled close. Though sometimes they woke up to make love before drifting back to sleep.

It was the crowing of the rooster that woke them the next morning. Mandy tried to smooth the wrinkles out of her long dress, while Night Wolf picked the hay out of her hair.

"Do you think they will know you spent the night here?" he joked at her disheveled condition.

"I don't care if the whole world knows," Mandy said with a pink glow to her cheeks. "Come up to the house and I'll make breakfast."

"Maybe I should go," he suggested, not certain

if his presence would be welcome.

"If we're going to be husband and wife there are plans to be made. And you will have to face them sooner or later."

John Jay was standing on the back steps with a hot cup of coffee in his hand. It was a crisp, cool morning so he had on his mackinaw. He didn't look surprised to see Mandy and Night Wolf come out of the barn, not after Abby's alert.

"Abby's fixing breakfast," he said, his gaze including Night Wolf. "You just have time to get washed up."

Night Wolf merely nodded in greeting as he went up the back steps. John Jay held the back door open for them, reaching out to pluck a bit of hay from Night Wolf's long hair. The two men exchanged knowing grins.

For Night Wolf, it was unusual to be in a white person's home, but he knew he needed to get used to it. He would not ask his wife to live in an ewa.

After washing up, they took their place at the table as Abby placed a platter of scrambled eggs, bacon and biscuits, along with fresh butter and apple sauce, in the middle of it.

Night Wolf had a little experience in the survey-ors' camp using a knife and fork. Mandy coached him without embarrassment.

"Where are the children?" Mandy asked, knowing they would usually be here at the table.

"Delfina and Danny are feeding them in the parlor." Her gaze rested on Night Wolf with a warm smile. "We thought you would be more comfortable with just us this morning."

"How did you know we'd...?" Mandy broke off, her cheeks flushing.

John Jay gave a soft laugh. "It wouldn't be the first time that hay was used for a bed." His eyes were dancing with mischief as he looked at Abby.

Then it was Abby's turn to blush. "There's something about the smell of fresh cut hay," she joked.

The meal passed pleasantly. In such friendly company Night Wolf wasn't embarrassed by Mandy's coaching on his table manners. "We wish to be married soon," he said to John Jay. "We don't know how to do this. And I wish to take a Spanish name."

"I think Vicenta Carrillo would be more than happy to have another wedding in their little chapel. I will write to her, and to Judge Hayes who can arrange the name change."

"Is good," Night wolf said, copying John Jay as he wiped his mouth with a napkin. "How soon?"

"I'll write the letters this morning. Brian Carter should be by with mail today or tomorrow."

The sound of the agitated clucking of chickens outside drew their attention to three riders approaching from the north. Abby recognized Marshall Lew Barker as they pulled up at the hitch rail and dismounted.

John Jay went out to greet them. "Marshall, you're out early."

As they shook hands the Marshall looked beyond him to Abby, Mandy and Night Wolf. John Jay introduced him to Night Wolf...who was wary.

"I've heard good things about you," the Marshall said as he shook hands with the tall Indian in buckskins.

Night Wolf merely nodded in greeting, relieved.

"I have a fresh pot of coffee, Marshall," Abby said. "You and your men are welcome to come inside."

"That would be mighty welcome, Mrs. Butterfield." He looked back to his two deputies. "You boys water the horses while I talk to these folks." Then to Abby he said, "Maybe the boys could have their coffee outside."

"I'll see to that," Mandy said.

The Marshall was invited to sit at the table and help himself to any leftover bacon and biscuits. His deputies were more interested in having Danny show them where to find the best apples.

"Glad you're here, Mr. Butterfield."

"Call me John Jay."

"John Jay, then."

Night Wolf and Abby sat at the table to listen, and Mandy soon joined them.

"There's a problem in the area that I'm not allowed to do anything about…because it involves Indians." His gaze rested on Night Wolf. "And just maybe you can help."

Night Wolf nodded to show he was interested.

"A young Indian girl has gone missing, maybe ten, twelve years old. She was out gathering acorns. Her basket was found, and it looked like signs of a struggle," He looked meaningfully at Mandy. "Those Basque sheep herders were in the area."

"Oh!" she gasped. "That sounds like something they would do. Did you confront them?"

The Marshall had a sheepish look. "Here's the thing, folks. If it was a white girl we'd be all over them…" He didn't need to finish. He could arrest an Indian for breaking the law, but a possible Indian kidnapping was out of his hands.

"Why did you come here?" Night Wolf asked.

"Because I was hoping to find someone who could take action," he stated, looking from Night Wolf to John Jay.

"Where are they?" John Jay asked.

"The herd was seen up by Overmeyer's Ranch."

"Overmeyer!" Abby and Night Wolf said at the same time. Abby spoke. "He's the one who had his vaqueros stampede cattle through my Kumeyaay Village, destroying it."

"It was just luck that no one killed," Night Wolf said, slipping back to his partial English.

"He's a mean one," the Marshall said. "But we've had more than a few complaints about someone elses sheep on his land."

John Jay looked at Night Wolf. "What do you say we go check that out?"

Night Wolf nodded enthusiastically.

"I'm going, too!" Mandy said. "I owe those bastard brothers! And especially if they've kidnapped that girl."

"I'll go, too," Abby said. "My medicine skills might be needed."

The Marshall stood up with a look of satisfaction. "Good luck. I'll be in the area. I'll call on Overmeyer with the excuse of listening to his complaints about the sheep."

15

It took several hours to prepare for what could be a week in the wilderness, with supplies for the four of them.

Abby took the time to write to Judge Hayes about Night Wolf's name change, and to Vicenta asking if the wedding could be held in her chapel.

Some of John Jay's clothes would fit Night Wolf, and he allowed Mandy to trim his hair, though most men in the back country wore their hair long. And with a used hat from one of the vaqueros, Night Wolf, at a glance, could pass for a vaquero.

Their first destination would be Overmeyer's ranch, and to then try to find the herd of sheep. They knew the Marshall would reach there ahead of them and hopefully help to cool the rancher's quick temper.

By the time they reached the ranch, Overmeyer's men were trying to force the large herd of sheep out of his pastures, heading them toward the San Filipe Valley and the Carrillo Rancho, a huge problem since Vicenta also had a large herd of sheep. Once intermingled, it would be impossible to separate them.

In the distance they could see Overmeyer shouting orders to his vaqueros and the Marshall and his two deputies standing by helplessly.

As John Jay and Night Wolf rode to catch up with the Basque brothers it was obvious exactly what the brothers were doing. By riding hard they tried to head off the sheep, while Abby and Mandy headed for the brothers' supply caravan. As they approached the large wagon, they could see the brother driving it was engaged in a fight with a young Indian girl, who had a rope tied around one wrist to keep her from escaping. It was a young girl Abby had seen before in a neighboring Kumeyaay village.

The girl saw her coming, and as Abby came up next to the caravan, she gave the brother one final vicious bite on the hand holding onto her rope and yanked free. She then leaped onto the back of Abby's horse. Mandy, riding on the other side of her, kept an eye on the brother to make certain he wouldn't try to reclaim his prisoner.

Ahead of them, John Jay and Night Wolf were heading off the confused herd of sheep. The three Basque brothers were trying to whip the animals into a frenzy, while Overmeyer's men flanked them to discourage any escapes. Once at the edge of Overmeyer's property his riders broke off. Except one of them turned his horse toward Mandy yelling excitedly.

"Mandy! Mandy!"

Mandy reined her horse sharply to stare at the approaching rider. "Tod!" He reined in next to her, was so excited to hug her they both tumbled from their horses into a heap of arms and legs on the ground. They talked over each other. "Where have you been?" her brother finally demanded. "I searched for you. The brothers said you were kidnapped by an Indian."

Just then Night Wolf rode up, angry to find a man entangled on the ground with his woman. Tod didn't know what to make of the furious Indian.

"Tod, this is Night Wolf, who rescued me from the brothers. You have no idea what they did to me once you were gone. This man helped me, he didn't kidnap me." She looked up at the glowering

Indian. "Night Wolf, this is my brother Tod." Then to her brother. "Help us!"

The anger left Night Wolf's face when he saw they did indeed share a family resemblance.

When Tod saw what they intended to do with the sheep, and realized how the brothers had mistreated his sister, he gave a whoop of excitement and leaped onto his horse and headed into the fray, followed closely by Night Wolf.

With guns firing in the air, John Jay and Tod were able to turn the stampeding sheep away from the Carrillo herd, and kept them headed into a rocky arroyo that would eventually lead them to the unoccupied lands of the San Filipe Valley.

Abby held the young girl tight until she could rein her horse in under the shade of an oak tree.

In a rush of words, the young girl thanked her as she sank down onto the cool ground in relief, and unfastened the rope from around her wrist. "You are Eagle Woman," she said recognizing the distinctive white wings at Abby's temples. "I am Anya. You saved me from those pigs!"

"Anya, did those men hurt you?" she asked in Kumeyaay.

"No! They try! I say I have white man's disease, so they make me cook and wash clothes."

Abby chuckled. "You are smart, Anya. Another woman wasn't so fortunate."

"Give me a knife! I make sure they don't take another!"

Abby couldn't help but laugh at the girl's courage. "We will return you to your village on our way back."

"I want to go home," she agreed. "But bad men go free!"

"Maybe for now," she said scowling. "Right now, they'll have enough trouble gathering up their scattered flock."

"Knife better!" Anya insisted as the rest of the party rode up.

They made camp there for the night. The next day they would return Anya to her village.

16

Night Wolf's scouts told him that the Zubiri brothers and their herd were still in the San Filipe Valley where they had set up camp, the sheep now grazing on open land, and that in the evening the brothers ate their supper outside their tent without weapons.

He gathered six young men eager for an adventure. In a grove of trees near the brothers' camp, they dismounted from their horses and then opened the robes of supplies they had brought. Talking excitedly, they prepared for their role. Stripping off their denim trousers and shirts, they put on loin cloths. From small pots they dabbed their faces and chests with war paint. Each one tied a band around his forehead and stuck turkey feathers in the back, and arranged his hair to hang long and straight. In the gathering twilight, they hoped the brothers wouldn't see beyond the paint and the costumes to the ages of the youths.

On foot, Night Wolf and his young band of would-be warriors silently approached the sheep men's camp, leading their horses. The four brothers were outside sitting around a fire, eating their supper. Only one rifle was visible, leaning against the opening to the tent, some twenty feet away. Clearly the brothers were not expecting trouble, which is what Night Wolf was counting on.

With only bows and arrows, the Indians mounted their horses, and with loud war cries rode toward the unsuspecting brothers. After the initial shock of being under attack by what looked to be a savage war party, Etienne knocked over his stool in a lunge for the rifle.

Night Wolf sent a spear whizzing past Etienne's head to imbed itself in the tent beside the rifle, knocking it over. There was mass confusion among the brothers. Realizing they were unarmed and helpless, they threw their arms up in the air in surrender.

Since he was the fiercest looking of the group, Night Wolf reined up close to Etienne, holding an arrow strung tight to his bow. "You steal girl!" he growled in his fiercest voice. "Second time you do this!"

"No! We didn't…"

"Silence!" Night Wolf ordered. "You lie! You do this again we come back with big war party."

The Zubiri brothers were cowering behind their oldest brother, clearly convinced they were going to die as the other Indians continued their war cries, shaking their bows threateningly.

"In payment!" Night Wolf barked. "We take five sheep to girl's family." He let that sink in. "Next time we scatter herd into the hills and burn your camp!"

With wild whoops the young Indians followed Night Wolf as he went out into the herd and selected five sturdy sheep, a male and four females. They drove them off into the darkening night, to the place where they had left their clothes.

The youths were laughing at how they'd scared the sheep herders, but Night Wolf took up his rifle to watch the herder's camp, making certain they wouldn't try to come after them. They wiped off the war paint and put their clothes on, then kept watch while Night Wolf did the same.

Well satisfied with the ruse, and the taking of the sheep, Night Wolf led the group in driving the sheep off into the night. It was little enough payment for the stealing of the girl. Her village was poor. The sheep would be a help. He couldn't wait to tell Mandy what they had done. He only wished there was some form of payment for what the brothers had done to her.

He doubted the brothers would be kidnapping any more women.

17

Several days later, Mandy was just finishing cleaning up the breakfast dishes. From the parlor came the sound of Abby reading to Jay and Ellie. John Jay and Danny were off into the fields, accompanied by their vaqueros. Her face lit up as she recognized the familiar bird call from outside.

Grabbing a shawl next to the back door, she hurried out, aware that her stomach was growing, and starting to limit her actions. In the barn, she stepped straight into Night Wolf's embrace. For a time they didn't speak, just absorbing the warmth of their bodies pressed together.

"Are you okay?" she asked. "Did the soldiers ever come to Green Valley?"

"No, the situation is settled now. Once Sotero's people heard the soldiers would be coming, they scattered." He gave her a sexy grin. "And I have to tell you what I did to those Basque brothers."

As he told her the story of the youths the Zubrinis thought to be a war party, Mandy laughed so hard she had to sit down on a bale of hay. "They thought you were a war party?"

Night Wolf grinned proudly. "Scared them good. I doubt they will be risking any more kidnappings."

"I'd love to have seen that," she said, still grinning.

"I'd like to have done more," he admitted. "But they aren't worth the risk of bringing soldiers." He sat next to her on the hay and drew her into his arms. "And you? How is it with you and your child?"

"He grows, he kicks."

"He?"

"Yes, Abby says it will be a boy."

"I have made a place for us in Green Valley. They look forward to having a teacher for the children." He regarded her seriously. "You think you can live there with me?"

"Oh yes! I would live anywhere with you," she cried as she burrowed into his embrace. "I can't wait. I can't wait to be your wife."

"I will take good care of you and our son. Everyone will think he is mine."

"Abby is arranging for the wedding at the Carrillo Rancho. I think a date has been set for two weeks from now," she said.

Night Wolf stood up and pulled her toward the fragrant pile of fresh hay where they had spent one glorious night making love. Mandy went with him eagerly. He tumbled her into the hay, and soon they had lost all track of time, or anything but having their bodies entwined together.

Abby pretended not to notice that Mandy's cheeks were flushed when she came in the back door. She had heard Night Wolf's whistle earlier and knew they needed time together.

Mandy began to strut about the kitchen with a hoity toity air. "I am going to live in a proper house on your Green Valley land, and I will be called Mrs. Sostenes Del Rio."

Abby laughed. "My, my, what a change that man has made, from renegade, to rancher, to husband and father."

"Everyone will think the baby is his. I can't wait to move there." But suddenly she looked at Abby, stricken by what her happiness would mean to her. "But...I will be leaving you."

"We both knew this was only temporary. You deserve your own life, and you are getting a very good man for your husband." Abby hugged her. "And don't worry, I have plenty of help. I have Delfina, and one of the vaqueros is taking a wife who has already said she wants to help me. I've known her since I was young."

Mandy looked relieved.

"Why did he choose that name?" Abby asked curiously. "I've never heard it before. Sostenes? What does it mean?"

"He tried to explain it to me. Sostenes is to sustain, to support. And Del Rio because he comes from the big river we call the Colorado," Mandy said as she picked up Ellie and nestled her playfully. Ellie giggled and plucked at Mandy's blonde hair.

Abby shook her head. "I can't imagine him as anything but Night Wolf. Who gave him that name?"

"He said in the hills near Warner Springs lives a very old man who once lived along the big river. He knew Night Wolf as a boy. He gave him the new name."

"Vicenta said everything is arranged for the wedding. It must be soon, before you are showing too much."

"Night Wolf has gone to talk to John Jay, to see if he can stay the night in your barn." Mandy flushed when she remembered how Night Wolf would not let her stay in the chilly barn with him.

"We have extra beds in the bunk house, and some of our vaqueros are Indian. He doesn't need to sleep in the barn," Abby said.

"I'm not sure he wants to be inside," Mandy said with a shrug.

"Well, it's something he's going to have to learn."

With the approach of the wedding, the initial awkwardness between John Jay and Night Wolf soon dissolved into friendship. During this time, Night Wolf underwent a transformation from Indian to vaquero. Among the stores of clothing, they found trousers to fit him, plus John Jay's shirts would fit, but no boots would fit his large feet.

"Bah! These feet are used to their freedom. I don't fit your boots," Night Wolf groused to Abby and Mandy.

"I think moccasins will have to do," Abby said. "I doubt anyone will care."

Mandy's family was invited. Her brother Tod now worked for John Jay and was more than happy to live in the bunkhouse and be near his sister.

They could always use an extra hand.

At the Carrillo Rancho, preparations were in full swing for the expected guests. Even if they didn't know the bride or the groom, many of them knew Jacob Bristol, or were just eager for a chance to party and to stage a rodeo. Vaqueros were always eager to show off their riding and roping skills.

Since the ranch house could not hold all the guests, many brought their own tents which were set up around the yard. One tent was set away from the others, decorated with desert holly and flowers from Vicenta's garden. The newlyweds could have shared a bedroom in the house, but with Night Wolf being unused to sleeping inside, they had chosen a tent.

"You have to get used to it sometime," Mandy teased him. "After all, you have had a house built for us."

"I will when I sleep in my own house, not some-one else's," he said holding her close to him as they sat in the back seat of the carriage taking them to the Carrillo's rancho. Behind them, Danny drove a second wagon with Tod and their supplies and tents.

Abby had been surprised to see Danny adding a guitar to his belongings in the wagon. A few times she had heard him singing to the children which kept them entertained for hours. And, at weddings, there was always music. It seemed to be a part of life for the vaqueros, be they Spanish or Mexican or White. At the ranchos, every event featured many instruments, guitars, fiddles, harmonicas, and sometimes drums. Even for the Indians, music was an integral part of their history. When Abby lived among the Kumeyaay, traditions were passed down in song.

Mandy could tell Night Wolf was nervous about all the people who would be there, of meeting her family and the many others who would come to see him wed the woman he loved. Indian ways were much simpler, but he could no longer live that life. Too much had changed. He had changed, though there were times when he wished he could don his buckskins, jump on his horse and disappear into the mountains... to hunt for his food and sleep under the stars. Now he was taking a white woman for a wife and would soon be a father to her child. And that, he found, he was eager to embrace.

The day before the wedding, Abby, John Jay, Night Wolf, Mandy and Tod were sitting out on the veranda with the Carrillos and other guests when new arrivals pulled into the yard.

Mandy and Tod looked at each other, unsure what to do as they recognized the Bristol family from Temecula: Jacob, their father; Louise their mother and their two brothers and one sister.

Night Wolf felt the tension in Mandy's body as he stood behind her chair, his hands resting on her shoulders as Jacob's stern gaze took in the tableau. He didn't even stop to help his wife down as he approached his runaway daughter, barely sparing Tod a glance.

Jacob studied the tall Indian standing behind his daughter, trying to reconcile his long held conviction about heathens with this handsome, well-dressed man.

One of the vaqueros helped Louise down, and the youngsters scrambled down on their own, seeking out children their own age. Louise went quickly to her husband and took his arm to remind him of her presence.

"Mandy," Louise said with tears in her eyes, "I'm so glad to see you safe and happy."

"Ma." Mandy was crying too. "I'm sorry I had to leave you."

"I know, child. I understood."

Mandy bolted from her chair into her mother's arms for a long hug. Then she looked at her father.

"Pa, I want you to meet my husband-to-be, Sostenes Del Rio." Her look into her father's eyes almost dared him to object.

Jacob's gaze went from Mandy to Night Wolf and back again. "But…he's…he's an Injun."

"Yes, he is," she said proudly. "From the Yuma tribe. And I shall be proud to call him husband."

Night Wolf stepped down from the porch with his hand outstretched. "I am pleased to meet the father and mother of my wife-to-be." His accent was slight, and for a moment Jacob looked from the tall man to his outstretched hand. He felt a nudge from his wife and slowly reached out. All his preconceived notions about heathen Indians were suddenly swept away.

"I'm thinking Mandy has picked herself a good man," Jacob managed to say. "I'm right pleased to make your acquaintance. This is my wife, Louise."

Everyone watching seemed to let out a sigh of relief. They hadn't been certain how Jacob would handle the situation.

Louise reached out to put her hand over Jacob's and Night Wolf's. "Welcome to the family…Sostenes, is it?" Louise asked.

"Yes, ma'am, Sostenes Del Rio."

Mandy placed her hand over her mother's,

then Tod stepped forward and placed his hand over Mandy's.

"Ma, Pa, it's good to see you," Tod said. "Good to feel like a family again."

Jacob's frown showed regret. "I'm sorry for driving you and Mandy away."

Their hands fell away, and then the afternoon celebration began. Food was brought out to the tables as more guests set up tents. When Judge Hays arrived, the first thing he did was take Night Wolf inside to the rancho's office, where he laid out the paperwork that would officially change his name. Night Wolf had practiced writing it many times in preparation, and now he proudly signed. He was now and forever, Sostenes Del Rio.

"Sostenes," Mandy said, hugging him, proud at the flourish with which he had signed his name.

18

Abby drew her shawl around her shoulders as she went out the back door carrying a basket to collect eggs from the hen house. It was a chore she enjoyed even if she had to endure a few pecks from an irate hen.

A storm had blown up suddenly out of the south, bringing strong winds and dark clouds. Later they would no doubt have rain. Maybe snow in the higher mountains around them.

Drawing the shawl closer for warmth, Abby entered the hen house, which was located on the south side of the barn. Something seemed to have disturbed the hens. Some were off their nests and clucking nervously. Possibly a predator of some sort. She talked to them soothingly as she collected the eggs, eight of them. Then, suddenly, whatever was disturbing them made the hair on the back of her neck stand up.

As she stepped out of the pen, she secured the latch, turning as a figure stepped out of the nearby grove of oak trees. Her eyes widened at the sight of a very angry Sotero, dressed in buckskins, his face painted in black lines, and in his hand a very sharp, wicked looking knife.

"I have waited two days to find you alone," he said angrily, approaching slowly, as if savoring the moment. "We will see which of us is stronger. I have heard of your Eagle powers."

Abby set the basket of eggs on the ground, taking one of them. She knew it would be useless to call for help. John Jay and Danny were in the fields securing everything for the expected high winds. If ever she needed her Eagle powers it was now as she stood unarmed, but unafraid.

"Your powers are weak, Sotero," she taunted him. "You have no medicine power. You have faked it for your people so they would choose you as their leader."

"Bah! Show me your power, woman," he taunted. "You will die here, and I will take your red hair as proof that I am stronger."

A sudden whirlwind swirled about them, raising a heavy cloud of dust. Abby threw the egg she held, striking Sotero right between his eyes so yolk and whites ran into his eyes.

"Aarrgh!" he yelled, wiping frantically to clear his vision. Looking thru a haze of splattered egg, he was ready to rush Eagle Woman and finish her, but she was no longer there.

A loud screech sounded from above him, sending his hair standing up in fear as pounding wings beat powerfully and a plummeting eagles' outstretched claws sank deep into his scalp. His knife flew out of his hand as he screamed in agony and tried to bat the eagle away. Blindly he ran back into the trees for his horse, hoping the tree limbs would knock the giant bird loose. His head was on fire. Talons sank deep. He beat at it with his fists, screaming. One talon slipped loose and raked across one eye. Even his horse was trying to get loose as Sotero jumped on his back and rode under low branches that forced the great bird to release its hold, screeching angrily. In moments Sotero disappeared into the forest of oaks, fleeing in terror from the furious bird.

John Jay heard the commotion and ran toward the sounds. He found Abby crumpled at the edge of the forest, her bonnet laying several feet away. A wicked looking knife lay nearby, but the only blood he saw was on her fingers. "Abby! Abby! What happened?"

Abby opened her eyes, disoriented. "Sotero," she whispered.

John Jay looked into the forest where he could hear a horse galloping away. "He's gone. Are you hurt?" He was frantic with worry.

Abby took stock of her body. The last thing she remembered was throwing an egg at Sotero, then things became fuzzy. She remembered screaming, no it was screeching, and had a vague, dream-like memory of grabbing onto Sotero's head, sinking in her talons.

"No," she murmured. "I'm not hurt. I...I'm not sure what happened."

"Well, he's gone. Let's get you up to the house before it starts to rain."

He helped her to her feet and she picked up her basket of eggs while he retrieved her bonnet and her shawl, wrapping it about her. Abby didn't try to recall what had happened to her. She only knew her spirit eagle had come to her rescue and sent her enemy fleeing for his life...with wounds that would forever disfigure him.

19

Long Bow was a rather short, squat man, well-muscled as most warriors were, though in recent years he had become more of a family man and used his warrior skills only to hunt for game to feed his family. Years ago he and his brother, Little Elk, had fled the Plains area when soldiers had attacked their village. Indiscriminately the soldiers shot women and children. He'd only had time to grab his younger brother and flee into a nearby canyon, hiding until there was only silence.

In the melee, Little Elk suffered a broken arm that had never healed properly. Now he was limited as to the weapons he could use, no rifle or bow and arrow, only a lance or a knife, or a throwing stick.

Fifteen-year-old Long Bow was already turning into a warrior, a smaller version of his father, a man who had hoped for peace between the Indians and the Whites. Yet they seemed to come in endless waves of wagon trains, seeking land, and often taking Indian land, which led to bitter fighting.

Once the soldiers were gone from their village that day they waited until dark before sneaking back. Every shadow scared them, taking the shape of a lurking soldier. But the utter silence scared them even more.

This night they were only frightened children as they walked through the burned out village. Dead bodies were everywhere. Men, women, and children. Even their dogs. Not one person had been spared. Teepees burned. Their stock driven off or slaughtered so there would be no food for survivors.

At that moment, Long Bow felt a wave of fury for the white soldiers who would do such a thing. It wasn't a battle of warrior against warrior. Even when Indians attacked, they rarely killed woman or children. Sometimes they would take them as slaves, but the women were rarely assaulted.

In the dark, Long Bow and Little Elk gathered up anything useful they could find and set out on foot to the nearest Lakota village, only to find it destroyed, too. Only a few youngsters like themselves had escaped. Banding together, they survived off the land, made weapons, and made war on any Whites they came across.

For many months the brothers rode the renegade trail, eventually making their way to California. They had met Night Wolf years earlier, when he also was a renegade, stealing horses from ranchos and from the Butterfield Overland Mail stations. Those horses brought the highest prices in Mexico due to their excellent condition. Strong horses were required to pull the stagecoaches.

The brothers found welcome at the Santa Ysabel Kumeyaay village, where eventually they each found a wife, and turned from their renegade ways.

Now, after many years, they ached to return to the land where they were born. Maybe they would find relatives at the Sun Dance, and could partici- pate in the rituals which were hundreds of years old, maybe more. It was a religious event consisting of prayer, personal vows, and sacrifice for the com- munity, as well as the singing and dancing in the sacred circle. It drew Indians from the Arapaho, Dakota, Lakota and Northern Cheyenne tribes.

Long Bow knew the warriors would try to keep the white soldiers from learning the loca- tion of the event. Indians who had already been forced onto reservations would be sneaking away to take part in the gathering, even though they knew soldiers would hunt them.

The journey was long. They followed the old Indian trails, but were cautious whenever they came across signs of white habitation.

At times they met other Indians on the trail and stopped to share news, camp together and share supplies.

For the children, it was a chance to play. For the wives, a chance to share stories and rest from the endless miles they had traveled.

If the others were also headed for the Sun Dance, they traveled together, sometimes sending a scout ahead to make certain the trail was safe.

At times they saw white settlements in the distance and became very cautious. In one area, they traveled only at night, hiding during the day until they were again in wilderness.

The two sons of Long Bow and Little Elk had become very accurate with throwing sticks, and often added fresh rabbit or squirrel meat to their meals.

In areas of lush vegetation, the women would gather anything edible. They lived off the land, and seldom went hungry. Plus, Indian trails took advantage of any available water, often from sources unknown to the Whites.

The gathering place at Rose Bud Creek for the Sun Dance was a huge grassy plain set against foot-hills on one side, and the creek on the other. Long Bow and Little Elk found a spot at the edge of the surrounding hills. They heard white soldiers had been seen in the area, and assisting them were their enemies, the Crow and Shoshone warriors.

Long Bow stood surveying the vast gathering of many well-known warriors and their clans.

"Look, Little Elk, there on the war ponies, two of our greatest warriors, Sitting Bull and Crazy Horse."

Little Elk stared at the mightiest of their clans. "But there are rumored to be many white soldiers not far from here."

"Our warriors will be watching them, but I chose this spot for us because we are close to a ravine. We will tell our women to take the chil-dren there if there is trouble."

"That is a good plan, brother. When we started this journey, we did not expect to see soldiers."

"It is said many of these warriors left their res-ervations to come here. The first thing we need to do is explore the ravine, perhaps use tumbleweeds to disguise the opening." They then talked to their families about what to do if soldiers came.

20

Long Bow gathered his weapons; a rifle, a lance, and a long hunting knife, picked the strongest of their horses and rode to where Sitting Bull and many warriors were gathered.

Sitting Bull was in council with Crazy Horse, and to Long Bow, it looked as if an attack on the white soldiers was being planned.

Since he was new to the situation, he dismounted and let his horse join several others grazing nearby. He greeted other warriors in a language he hadn't used in many years.

"I am Long Bow, born to the Sioux Nation, now with the Kumeyaay in the west."

The warriors returned his greeting with their clan names, some coming from almost as far as Long Bow to take part in the ceremonies of the Sun Dance.

"I am called Swift Fox," one said. "Soldiers

have been seen coming this way on the other side of the river. Chief Sitting Bull is calling on all warriors to arm themselves. We will ride out before they get too close to our camp."

"They are a threat to our women and children," Dark Moon added.

The sound of pounding hoof beats drew everyone's attention as a lone warrior rode up on a sweaty horse, going straight to the chiefs.

"White soldiers come!" the warrior said so all could hear. "There are many, but not yet ready to attack. They have stopped to rest their horses."

"Then we ride now!" Crazy Horse shouted.

"We go!" Sitting Bull agreed.

The camp erupted in war cries as a giant force of Sioux and Cheyenne gathered their weapons, mounted their war ponies and headed up the valley of Rosebud Creek. The thick vegetation growing along the creek, on both sides, would hide their approach, but it also concealed their enemy from them.

Within minutes, Long Bow was riding near the front of the mass of warriors. The Indians were well equipped for hand-to-hand combat with lances, tomahawks, knives and war shields. In addition they were armed with a number of fire arms, from muzzle loaders, to Spenser, Sharps, Henry, and the Winchester repeating rifles that held many bullets.

Ahead of them, Long Bow saw the Indian scouts for the soldiers turn tail and flee from the approaching force. But, it was almost too late for the soldiers to prepare. They hadn't realized the Indian camp was so close and had been caught by surprise.

The Crow and Shoshone, Indian allies of General Crook, formed an advanced position ahead of the main body of soldiers, and took the brunt of the attack. This gave General Crook's men time to get mounted and charge forward to help.

Long Bow fired his rifle but bullets were few, the guns impossible to reload while on horseback. Soon he switched to bow and arrows at which he had always excelled.

He saw Chief Sitting Bull urging his warriors to fall back, and grinned at the wily chief's plan. He knew Chief Crazy Horse and his warriors had held back and the plan was to draw the soldiers into an ambush.

On Crook's part, there were disconnected actions and counter charges. The battle front grew to three miles wide, impossible to command, when each man was fighting for his life.

The charging warriors were well trained in warfare. They provided little in the way of a target when they hung onto their horse with one hand, one leg over the horses back, and firing or hurling lances from under the horse's necks.

When General Crook found himself being attacked from three sides he ordered his men to withdraw. A bugle sounded the order. But it was Crook's Indian allies who largely saved the day. It was they who understood the Indian's way of warfare, while the soldiers did not.

With the arrival of additional troops, the battle raged on many fronts. A direct assault on the Indians would scatter them, only to have them regroup.

By mid-afternoon, the battle was over. Crook and his army quit the field, hopelessly outnumbered. They headed north in the direction of a place called Goose Creek, where his main camp was located.

∼

Long Bow's mount was exhausted, and so was he, as the warriors headed back to their camp.

A few scouts stayed behind to follow the soldiers and make certain they didn't turn around. Other warriors took scalps from dead soldiers and displayed them proudly as they rode in, while others gathered up spent arrows and lances, and any weapons and ammunition the soldiers had abandoned.

Knowing his family would be worried, Long Bow rode directly to their teepees. His son took his tired horse, knowing how to care for it, as Long Bow was welcomed like the returning warrior he was.

The following day, the Sun Dance ceremonies began. A main lodge was constructed around a tree the men had chopped down as part of the ritual, each man taking a turn with the ax.

A grassy area was marked as sacred, used only for the dancers who appeared in full regalia of eagle feathers, furs and beads.

Drummers surrounded one large drum, each blow falling as one, and the traditional, very ancient songs were sung.

Gourds had been turned into rattles as a cacophony of ritual music filled the air.

Long Bow had donned his treasured ceremonial regalia of elaborate deer skin moccasins, with beaded leggings and loin cloth. A beaded headband across his forehead held in place a headdress with many eagle feathers. His chest and face painted, he joined in the dancing, moving to the beat of the drummers and singers. His wife, Juanita, in a ceremonial deerskin dress stood at the edge of the sacred area with their son White Owl, whose regalia was not as ornate as his father's but he never-the-less mimicked the moves of the many dancers.

Beside her, Little Elk's wife, Spotted Fawn, also stood in ceremonial dress, and watched as her son joined White Owl at the edge of the dancers, learning too.

Somewhere amidst the many dancers, Long Bow knew his younger brother would be dancing like any warrior, perhaps forgetting for once the crippled arm that kept him from joining the battle.

The drums were the heartbeat of the Sun Dance. "We sing to our ancestors," they chanted.

"O, our Father, the Sky, Hear us and make us strong.

O, our Mother, the Earth, Hear us and give us support.

O, Spirit of the East, Send us your wisdom.

O, Spirit of the South, May we tread your path

of life.

O, Spirit of the West, May we always be ready for the long journey.

O, Spirit of the North, Purify us with your cleansing winds."

It was a proud moment for all the Indians that day. The Sun Dance was the greatest of the gatherings, and had drawn thousands of families from all over the Plains, and thousands of warriors to protect them, especially with the news of more soldiers coming from several different forts.

As for the generals, they hadn't realized the significance of the Sun Dance, and could only assume such a huge gathering was for the purpose of making war. General Crook withdrew his shattered forces to Fort Laramie, where he waited for reinforcements. This meant he and his troops were not in their assigned place when other troopers began converging on the Little Big Horn River, a fact that could very well have made all the difference in the events to come.

21

Abby sat in a comfortable old rocking chair that had rocked generations of Butterfield children. Her daughter had finally fallen asleep. Here in the large Butterfield home in Utica, New York, several generations had gathered for Ellen Louise Butterfield's first birthday party. Overly excited by the gathering and a large birthday cake with one candle, Ellie had trouble falling asleep. John Jay's mother, Malinda, had recommended the old rocking chair.

The parlor on the first floor was dark except for one lamp, and the house quiet for all the families who had gathered for the arrival of John Jay from far off California.

Four year old Jay, had loved the sea voyage, and had quickly discovered every nook and cranny of their passenger steam ship, which had traveled around the tip of South America.

Abby and John Jay had discussed the best way to deliver the survey plats and other records to President Grant, and decided on a sea voyage for the safe transport of a steamer trunk full of information, rather than trains. This way, there was no need for the trunk to be moved about, even though it took up a lot of space in their small cabin. A second stateroom had been secured for Delfina and the children.

Danny, too, enjoyed the long voyage and though he tried to keep track of Jay, he also found friends his own age. Every facet of the large steam ship fascinated him, and he spent time with any crew member who would take the time to explain the workings of the ship.

Little Ellie had not fared so well and was often sea sick. Delfina's Indian background had not prepared her for such a voyage, but she was curious about everything and a big help dealing with Ellie. She was able to use some of the herbs Abby always carried to help ease the nausea.

John Jay found some old friends among the other passengers and spent time exchanging stories. Everyone had heard about the Butterfield Overland Mail, and were fascinated by John Jay's stories of that first run from St. Joseph, Missouri to San Francisco in 25 days. Especially fascinating was the time when around three hundred Comanche warriors stopped the coach. John Jay, his shotgunner, and one passenger waited tensely in the shade of a nearby tree while the Indians inspected every inch of the coach and horses. They climbed inside the coach, inspected the lamps, the window shades, laughing as they did so. Their laughter made a very tense John Jay hopeful that this was no war party. After about three hours, one of the chiefs came over to them. "You go!" he said in English. "Go swift!"

The three men wasted no time mounting the coach and continuing on their way. The swift wagon was what the Indians called the red Concord stagecoach.

The Butterfield family arrived safely in New York City and took a local train to Utica. Already waiting for them were John Jay's three brothers and three sisters and their families, where they had gathered in the two story mansion built by John Butterfield Senior. Since Malinda Butterfield, John Senior's widow, could no longer climb the stairs to the second floor, her youngest son and his family had taken it over on a permanent basis. There

were enough bedrooms on the second floor to accommodate most of the large family, though some
spaces were a bit cramped.

John Jay and Abby and the two youngsters
had a bedroom down stairs, while Delfina shared
quarters with a maid hired especially for this
huge gathering. When she returned to California
she would have many stories to tell her Indian
grandchildren.

Danny was perfectly happy to bed down in a
corner of the parlor, or share space with one of
his new cousins. He spent a lot of time with them,
learning about their schooling or professions, which
greatly enhanced his view of the world. He began
to see there could be opportunities for him here.

John Senior had many business interests, of
which the Butterfield Overland Mail had been
only a small part. Though at first the $600.000
a year mail contract seemed enormous, in the
end the mail was deeply in debt. Keeping remote
stations stocked with man power, horses and supplies, maintaining roads and water wells, fighting
off marauding Indians and bandits had taken a
huge toll of the company's expenses. When the
Civil War broke out, it interrupted the flow of
mail due to its southern route and the Butterfield

Overland Mail shut down its operation. In the end, John Senior had still been a wealthy man, and his sons now ran many of the remaining family businesses.

John Jay's brother, Daniel had served with the Union Army as a brevet Major General during the Civil War, and was now Assistant US Treasurer under President Ulysses S. Grant. During his time in the military, Daniel created the mournful trumpet call played at military funerals ever since. It was called "Taps." And with Daniel's familiar presence in the White House it would assist John Jay and Abby in delivering the survey plats and treaties directly to the President. Too many treaties had disappeared in the past to risk any other method. President Grant readily agreed.

"Is she asleep?" John Jay whispered to Abby, gazing fondly at his finally silent daughter.

"Yes, but I've been afraid to move," Abby said.

"Let me take her." Carefully John Jay lifted Ellie into his arms. For a moment she fussed, and Abby held her breath. Then Ellie settled into John Jay's arms and he carried her into their bedroom and settled her in her crib. Jay was already asleep on a pallet in the corner.

With the big house filled with family, there were

no separate rooms for the children.

Two days later, Abby, John Jay and Daniel boarded the Utica Railroad, the start of their journey to Washington D.C. With them was the large steamer trunk that held the survey plats for President Grant. In New York City they switched trains, always keeping their eyes on the precious trunk. At the D.C. station, a carriage awaited them for the ride to the White House.

John Jay watched the changing scenery as they approached the White House, and though he had visited the White House during his father's illness urging the President to honor the Indian treaties, he hadn't known much about the man. He had heard that Grant once served with the military in California, so he asked his brother.

"Did you serve with Grant in the war?"

"No, not directly," Daniel answered. "We had separate commands."

"I remember hearing his name in California before the war. What did he do there?"

"Well, first of all, he was a graduate of West Point, and during the Mexican-American War, he was a lieutenant. After that, he was in San Francisco, then at Fort Vancouver in the Pacific Northwest," Daniel said. "He once told me he found the native people he encountered to be harmless. It was the whites who caused most of the problems by bringing whisky and small pox and by coveting their land."

Abby was scowling at his words. She, too, had witnessed similar problems, having lost her Kumeyaay parents to small pox.

"Later," Daniel went on. "Grant was stationed at Fort Humboldt in Northern California, made Captain by then, but got in trouble for drunkenness. He was given a choice, resign or be court marshalled. Of course, he resigned."

"I never heard about that," John Jay said. "So how did he get to be a General?"

"The Civil War," Daniel said. "There was a call for 75,000 volunteers in Galina, Illinois, his home. And being a former Captain, he was the only professional in Galina. He worked with Major John C. Fremont, who proclaimed Grant a man of dogged persistence and iron will."

"But by March 1869, after President Andrew Johnson was impeached, Grant became the eighteenth president of the United States," John Jay added.

"I know he helped some of the California Indians after that," Abby said. "Granting two reservations in Northern California, so we can only hope he will see this situation as becoming critical, with so many lost records."

"You'll find him receptive to your reservations," Daniel explained. "But not everyone in Congress feels as he does. If he were to take those proposed reservations to them, you can bet there'd be a long delay while it's debated to death and most likely, in the end, no decision reached. That's the way it's been for a hundred years." As they neared the White House, Daniel continued. "I'm hoping the President will limit the discussion to his Cabinet... since previous treaties had a way of disappearing after being sent to Congress."

"I find that very discouraging," Abby said with a deep frown. "How could they all vanish as if they never existed?"

"And the Indians waited and waited for promises that were never fulfilled," John Jay added.

It was a mild summer day in early June. Abby wore a light weight mint green gown without all the usual petticoats some fashions required. It had short puffy sleeves and a small hat was perched to one side over her upswept red hair. The white wings at each of her temples stood out in the heat.

At the White House side entrance, two porters

were waiting with a hand wagon to transport the trunk to the President's office. President Grant had agreed to have it where he could see it, and watch over it so that it didn't vanish as so many had before.

Daniel led John Jay and Abby to the main doorway into the office of the President. The two security guards were expecting them. Robert Lewis and Albert Jenkins knew Daniel from previous visits, and were also military, having served with General Grant in the Civil War. Out of habit they saluted since the two had known Daniel as Major General Butterfield. Then they opened the doors to announce the visitors.

Grant came forward from his large desk, shaking hands first with Daniel, then John Jay as they were introduced, and then Abby. He was an imposing figure with his tailor-made blue suit, and neatly trimmed beard and moustache. His blue eyes were piercing in their intensity, and direct as he took Abby's hand, staring in fascination.

"My dear," he said. "I am honored to meet you. I've been told how you made this survey possible due to your relationship with the local Indians. My friends in San Diego said it could not have been done without your help."

"I am honored to meet you, sir," Abby said, feeling the warmth of his hand in hers.

His gaze swung to John Jay as he released her hand. "I knew your father, John Jay. An amazing man, as is your brother, my Assistant Treasurer."

"I'm honored, sir," John Jay said.

Grant got right down to business, looking at the steamer trunk that was sitting beside his desk. He had agreed to accept delivery of the plats and keep them until such time as they were worked into his busy schedule.

"So this contains the latest survey plats?"

"Yes, sir," John Jay answered. "And two new treaties the San Diego Indian Agent sent."

Grant waved them into three chairs arranged in front of his large mahogany desk, then he took his chair behind it and pressed a button.

A side door opened and two men in white jackets pushed a tea cart into the room, served first the President, then the three visitors. Silently they left the room the way they had come, leaving the tea cart behind.

After one sip of the cool, sweet tea, Grant was ready to talk business. "I've raised holy hell with Congress over the missing treaties, but it hasn't done a bit of good. There are such mixed feelings about the Indians. Some think they should be granted land to compensate them for what we've already taken away. Others think they should be exterminated. As a result they don't agree on anything."

Abby spoke up. "Because so much land has been taken from them already, these families can no longer live in their traditional ways. In the past, they would move several times during the year to where food was available. Few of them planted crops for that same reason and this kept their villages from becoming too large." She paused to take a sip of her tea, aware the President was listening intently. "Now, because they are mostly restricted to only one place, many have sought employment with the ranchers, as vaqueros, and as household staff. They have learned to plant gardens."

"I've been deeply troubled by the way these first Americans have been treated. During the war, I had occasion to hire several Indians as scouts, and for help around our camps. I don't agree with the opinion of too many congressmen that they are incapable of learning our ways, and are little more than animals. They claim it's not worth granting good land for reservations."

"It's not that they are incapable," Abby said. "They only want the freedom to live as they always have, to practice their own beliefs and not be forced to accept the white man's ways or his God."

Grant nodded. "Some Whites just won't believe they don't wish to become like us, be absorbed by us with our superior White beliefs. We're having the same problem now that Negros are free. There is a great deal of prejudice against them."

"I've been hearing about this Ku Klux Klan," John Jay said. "And their violence against blacks."

"Yes," Grant said with a scowl. "Men wearing bed sheets, dispensing their version of justice against the slightest perceived insult. Often at the end of a rope."

"Bad business," John Jay said.

"And other Whites are protecting their identities. You can't punish them if you don't know who they are," Daniel added.

"But, back to the Indian problem," Grant said. "I will be meeting with my Cabinet this afternoon, and I will make it clear to them that the plats and treaties will not leave my possession until a decision has been reached. You can expect to hear from me in about two weeks."

After exchanging pleasantries, the three visitors took their leave. Since Abby knew little about the Capital, and John Jay only had short visits in the past, Daniel gave them a guided tour.

From the White House, they strolled along a tract of land set aside for memorials to the nation and to various presidents.

"They call this the Mall," Daniel said, playing tour guide. "The building in the distance, hidden by scaffolding, will be the Washington Monument. I've seen drawings of what it will look like in maybe another five years. Amazing."

"Just what we're seeing is amazing," Abby said, her attention directed to the Smithsonian Institution.

"That's sometimes called The Castle," Daniel said. "It's an art gallery, a library, a chemical laboratory, and also has lecture halls, museum galleries and offices. My wife and I often attend lectures here."

"I can see the Potomac River," John Jay said looking across the tidal basin.

"It's a beautiful site," Daniel said as they turned back to the White House where their carriage waited. "Someday there'll be gardens and memorials for all the presidents. I've already seen a proposal for the Lincoln Memorial. But, that's in the future, after the Washington Monument is completed."

The return to Utica the next day, after spending

the night with Daniel and his wife Julia in D.C. was uneventful. Abby had missed the children, and they were excited to see her and John Jay. Daniel had remained in D.C. and would contact them by telegram when he had news.

"The little ones missed you," Grandma Malinda said, "but with Delfina's help we've been able to keep them amused. And, it's given me a chance to get to know them. With you being so far away in California, I won't see much of them."

"I know," Abby said. "We're a long ways from here."

"Well, I've heard California is a wonderful place to live. No snow to shovel."

Malinda Butterfield was still a handsome woman in her 80s. Her son Warren and his family had taken over the upstairs portion of the house since Malinda could no longer manage the stairway. With one fulltime cook and housekeeper, she managed very well. But right now, with additional family crowding every available space for John Jay's visit, she enjoyed the sound of laughter filling her house again, and children of various ages playing. She thoroughly enjoyed her role as grandmother.

With the addition of Delfina, and the temporary

maid, Susie, they were managing the large meals and housekeeping for the entire family quite well.

22

Danny was enjoying the company of two of his newly discovered cousins Donald and Marty, both about his age. He was learning something new every day while the boys were on a semester break from their Academy in Maryland.

When Delfina and Susie took Ellie and Jay to a nearby park, the three young men trailed along with a baseball to play catch. His cousins were encouraging him to stay and attend their school. But, since Danny had never attended a regular school, his only knowledge was only what Abby had been teaching him. He doubted he would fit in.

"Tell you what," Marty said. "My Dad is a professor, let's ask him to test you to see if you can qualify."

Danny was eager for that, and was now becoming more adept at throwing the large pigskin covered ball. Baseball was becoming more popular at the schools.

Jay was playing on the swings with Susie's help, while Delfina was walking along a pathway lined with rose bushes pushing Ellie in a carriage. The two were fascinated by the colorful array of flowers.

As Danny enjoyed the company of his cousins, he wondered if he could truly fit in here, attend school, and work in one of the family businesses. And, would Abby and John Jay allow him to stay? If he felt he was truly needed at Eagles' Rest he would go back with them, but this was an opportunity he might never have again. And, if he were in California, what would he do when he was older? Someday he'd want a wife and family. How would he support them?

"Oh oh," Donald said, looking beyond Danny. "Here comes trouble."

Glancing over his shoulder, Danny saw four boys about their age coming straight for them, and everything in their posture said trouble. "Who are they?" he asked, no stranger to trouble since his homeless days in Los Angeles.

"Homer Stanton and his gang. He's been pissed ever since the Amherst Academy accepted us and turned them down."

"Why were they turned down?" Danny asked, but guessed the reason even before Donald spoke.

"He's a trouble maker and a liar. The school checked him out and said no, so now they go to a school here in Utica."

The four boys stopped up close to Danny and his cousins, but their attention was clearly on Danny with smug smiles.

"I hear your mama's a squaw," Homer said, looking at Delfina, whose dark skin and full figure plainly spoke of her heritage.

Rather than show anger, Danny smiled. "I'd be right proud to call Mrs. Delfina my mother. She's a Kumeyaay Indian, and a grandmother who helps my family."

"She take scalps?" the pale, blonde boy asked.

"Probably would if she were riled," Danny said calmly.

"How about you?" Homer asked. "You ever taken any scalps?"

Donald and Marty shifted uncomfortably, not sure what to do. It was obvious Homer and the gang wanted a fight, having the advantage of four of them against three.

"Well, now," Danny drawled, mimicking some of John Jay's mannerisms. "I could…if I had a reason."

He reached down into his boot and came up with a long-bladed hunting knife. "Where I come from," Danny went on as all six boys stared at it. "Everyone carries a knife. You never know when you might come across a bandit, or maybe a rattlesnake."

Suddenly Homer and his gang were not so sure of themselves. They'd never been faced with a weapon before.

Expertly Danny moved the knife from one hand to the other, making it obvious he knew how to handle it. "Yeah," he went on patiently. "My mother was raised by Indians after her parents were killed. She knows their ways, and is called a medicine woman. Between her and my dad, John Jay Butterfield, they've taught me how to protect myself. So I'm real good with a knife."

Donald and Marty were trying to keep from smirking, aware their new cousin was really putting the bullies on, and that they didn't quite know what to make of him. Their harassment wasn't going as planned. With four against three, they thought they had the advantage, but the sharp blade, and Danny's lack of fear had them stymied.

Danny made a point of studying Homer's full

head of dark brown hair. "You know, I don't have any scalps here in New York, and none that color. Mine are all back in California." He paused and let that sink in, and used the sharp blade to cut a strip of bark from a nearby tree. "Let me show you how we do it."

He took a step toward Homer, knife poised, his gaze fastened on Homer's pride and joy, his full head of hair.

"Dirty injun!" was all the insult Homer could come up with as his hand went to his head to protect it. He turned away in a hurry and his buddies followed.

Donald and Marty were smothering their laughter until Homer and his gang were gone, then they burst out laughing.

Danny looked around, hoping no one else had seen his charade, and saw only one elderly man limping by, a crooked smile on his lips. He knew a successful bluff when he saw one.

With his knife safely out of sight again in his boot, Danny and the boys returned to their ball throwing.

"So, how do you take scalps?" Marty asked in between gusts of laughter.

"Darned if I know," Danny said. "My Mom's

Kumeyaay tribe never took any."

Donald and Marty laughed all the harder, and their new cousin was definitely now one of the family.

That evening, after dinner, Donald's father, Warren, approached John Jay in the back yard. "I guess you heard about Danny today,"

John Jay grinned. "Yep, I'm right proud of that boy."

"He's a sharp lad, and Donald said he might like to stay here, come live with us. And if he qualifies, attend the same academy as my son."

John Jay's grin faded at this unexpected news. "You think he'd qualify?"

"Well, I sort of tested him out, knowing he's never been to a real school. And I was surprised that except for math, he was close to qualifying for Amherst. I can tutor him, and I think he'll pass the test by next semester. In the meantime, he wants to work for me at the telegraph company."

For a long moment John Jay was silent, thoughtful. He'd long been aware of Danny turning into a man, and with few prospects in California.

"Warren, this sounds like a perfect opportunity for Danny. I've been concerned for his future and I really appreciate the fact you're willing to take responsibility for him."

"He's an exceptional young man. My boys like him. I think I'll be gaining one very good worker," he paused a moment then a playful glint came into his eyes. "But we may have to do something about that knife he carries. Amherst would definitely frown on that."

John Jay laughed. "Okay, let me talk to him, and my wife. I'll have to convince her this is for the best. We'll have an answer for you tomorrow.

Abby saw the smile on John Jay's face after his talk with his brother, and knew something important was in the wind.

23

Two weeks passed with no word from President Grant. Daniel remained in D.C. waiting to hear, and sent Abby and John Jay telegrams every few days to let them know he was staying close.

Abby had been slow to accept the news about Danny. Slow to accept that even without her input, a plan had been worked out for him. As a mother, she felt she should have been consulted. But she acknowledged that Danny was no longer a child, and deserved the chance to find his own future.

It was obvious he had become fast friends with his cousins, and she respected John Jay's brother and his wife for being willing to accept this new responsibility. Returning to California without him would not be easy.

John Jay, Warren and Donald took Danny

shopping for clothes more suited to his new way of life. His work clothes from the ranch would not do here, nor the sturdy boots that held his weapon. A smaller hat replaced his broad brimmed work one.

"And who is this handsome young man?" Abby asked when Danny walked into the house in gray slacks, a pin striped white shirt and a light weight gray jacket, similar to the clothing worn by his cousins.

"My lady," John Jay said with a flourish. "May I introduce Master Danny Butterfield?"

Abby gave a curtsey. "I'm most happy to make your acquaintance, but I fear for the young ladies of New York."

Danny was grinning in embarrassment by all the attention. "Uncle Warren told me I can't carry my knife any more. And, besides, with shoes instead of boots, I don't have any place to carry it."

"Hopefully you won't be needing it here," John Jay said. "Gentlemen don't go around with weapons."

"Something I'll have to get used to," Danny said with a frown at this new image of himself. "I feel naked without it."

Danny and his new family would be leaving the next day to return to their home in New York City.

The new semester would be starting at Amherst and Donald and Marty needed to be there.

The parting scene was a sad one for Abby and John Jay. Danny had been a part of their lives for many years, and it was difficult to imagine life at the ranch without him. New York was so far away. They didn't know when they would see him again.

Danny, too, had tears in his eyes as he gave Abby a last hug, then climbed into the large carriage that would take them to the railway station.

Blindly, Abby went into John Jay's arms, tears streaming down her cheeks. His eyes were moist too as he hugged Abby tightly and watched the carriage pull away.

24

Corporal David Lewis was part of the 7th Cavalry under the command of General George Custer. He knew a three-pronged attack was planned on the Indians who were said to be gathering somewhere near the valley of the Little Big Horn River.

Another column marching north from Fort Fetterman in Wyoming Territory was led by General George Crook. And, General Gibbon's column was coming east from Fort Ellis in Montana Territory, as well as General Terry from Fort Abraham Lincoln in Dakota Territory. General George Custer was part of General Terry's forces.

Due to the large distance involved, and no reliable communications, Corporal Lewis knew that making any battle plan would be difficult. For that reason, the routes had been laid out in advance.

The only information they had on the Indians was that a large force was thought to be gathered in the area of Rosebud Creek. They presumed it was with hostile intent, and they hoped to take them by surprise.

Corporal Lewis's 7th Cavalry had been created just after the Civil War, and many men were veterans of that war, including most of Custer's officers.

Lewis had joined late in the big war, due to his young age, and had seen only one skirmish, which had lasted only a few hours. Whenever possible, he had written to his uncle Robert Lewis, who was an aide to President Grant, and who had fought many battles during the Civil War. Recently Lewis had returned from eighteen months of constabulary duty in the Deep South, then was recalled to Fort Abraham Lincoln to join the regiment for this campaign.

He couldn't help but wonder about the officer shortage in Custer's command, with only 45 officers assigned to 718 troops. This was a chronic shortage due to the Army's rigid seniority system. To help compensate for this, Custer had surrounded himself with family; his brother, Captain Tom Custer; a brother-in-law, Lieutenant James Calhoun; his youngest brother, Boston Custer; and a nephew, seventeen year old

Harry "Autie" Reed.

As the army neared the gathering of Indians, Custer ordered "No more trumpet calls."

Each trooper carried a hundred rounds of ammunition for his carbine, twenty-four rounds for his pistol, plus twelve pounds of oats for his horse. They were paid $13 a month. Extra ammunition and supplies were carried by the mule train following behind.

Corporal Lewis was with a small group of men under the cover of the thick growth of brush along the Little Big Horn River. He was with General Custer, his Indian scouts, and a few hand chosen men. Secretly, Lewis thought Custer had chosen him because his uncle was on President Grant's personal security team.

Leaving their horses hidden, the six of them moved thru the trees where they could look down on the village from a place called Crow's Nest. Looking across the Little Big Horn River, Lewis saw only women preparing food for the day, and young boys taking what looked like thousands of horses out to graze.

A raw wind was sweeping out of the northwest. Where June was usually a hot and dusty month, this year had proved different, the men all wearing their warmest uniform jackets.

Inaccurate information provided by Indian scouts, said no more than eight hundred hostiles were in the area, but they hadn't taken into account the many thousands of Indians who had left their reservations to attend the sacred Sun Dance.

With so few warriors visible, Custer remarked that the warriors must still be asleep in their teepees.

"We need to keep an eye on them," Custer said. "Get a better idea of how many there are." Even with the cold wind, Custer's face was sun-burned, his reddish bristles of a moustache standing out stiffly. He was wearing his usual outfit made of white buckskin pants and jacket, and a large white hat. He was well aware of the image he wanted to create when he later sent his dispatch to the New York Herald about the upcoming battle.

He sent Lewis and two other men back to their camp for supplies. Automatically the men scouted the area, looking for tracks of any hostiles, and were disconcerted when they found them. It was apparent the warriors in the village would soon be aware of their force.

When Lewis went back to Custer to report the tracks, the General was afraid the village would scatter and he would have to give chase. They rushed back to the main camp and geared up for an immediate attack.

Long Bow was fully prepared for the battle riding with Sitting Bull's main force, while Crazy Horse's warriors went to engage another approach of the soldiers. Their main goal was to protect the women and children, to keep the battles as far from them as possible.

It hadn't been easy for Long Bow to convince Little Elk to remain with the women and children, to protect them from a surprise attack. The warriors suspected the soldiers would try to take their encampment and take the women and children captive. But underneath that fear, Long Bow knew, was the fear their families would be killed instead.

There were women who would fight, elderly warriors too, and youngsters, all would help to repulse any attempt to capture them. And Little Elk was charged by his warrior brother to keep both their families safe.

As Little Elk and the two families watched the warriors ride out to meet the approaching soldiers, the women's faces were etched with worry. He knew what he had to do. Their teepees were not close to others since Long Bow had chosen this particular location.

"Gather food and blankets," he told his wife and Juanita. "We must move from here."

The women reacted and the boys helped, while Little Elk held his pistol and listened for any signs of battle. When it came, it was terrifying to hear. A steady barrage of gunfire.

He could hear the war cries of warriors, and his own heart was hammering with fear as he collapsed their two teepees and they retreated into the ravine. The boys helped him put brush in the opening to hide it. Then, while the two women and the children retreated to an alcove of sorts Long Bow had selected, Little Elk crouched by the entrance, hidden, watching. His heart pounding like a drum at the far off sounds of battle. He chanted a prayer to keep his brother safe.

On that morning of June 25, Custer gave orders to his troops, dividing his twelve companies into three battalions. Three companies were placed under the command of Major Marcus Reno, three under the command of Captain Frederick Benteen, and five companies under Custer's own command.

The 12th Company under Captain Thomas McDougall was assigned to escort the slower pack train to protect their provisions and ammunition.

Captain Benteen would take his troops to the right to cut off any Indians fleeing in that direction. Major Reno's battalion was sent down the left side of the Little Big Horn River to cut off any escape in that direction. Custer and his battalion would cross the river and hit the village straight on.

It was no secret to Lt. Lewis that Custer would try to hit the village first and capture all the glory for himself. It was not long past dawn when the full command began its three pronged attack on the village.

Lewis was tired; his horse was tired. The troopers had traveled all night behind General Custer, who was noted for his night travels, hoping to catch the Indians by surprise. But David Lewis didn't think that was a good strategy. The men and horses arrived tired and hungry.

Right now, he was under the direct command of Major Marcus Reno, whom he had seen taking more than a few sips from a flask under his shirt.

Major Reno advanced across an open field towards the north west, using the cover of trees and brush lining the banks of the Little Big Horn

River. But while the trees shielded him, it also obscured his view of the Indian encampment.

When he suddenly came into an open area, he could see a large cloud of dust in the distance where the village was located, and suddenly realized he was at the south end of a huge village, far larger than he had expected.

Seeing that a battle was clearly in the offing, the soldiers began to cheer and make their weapons ready.

"Stop that noise!" Reno shouted, then gave the next order. "Charge!"

Lewis thought Reno's words sounded slurred, and more than once he again saw their leader raise the flask to his lips.

But the troops followed their orders and charged toward the swirling dust cloud still too far ahead to use their weapons.

Lewis saw their Arikara scouts break off from the attack and head for the herd of Indian ponies.

Ahead of them, Lewis began to make out the village and a number of mounted warriors whose attention seemed to be aimed in the opposite direction. The gunfire told him the Indians were being attacked from that direction, probably by Custer.

He could see panic in the village as women and children sought safety along the river bed. And one of the leaders of the warriors in his war paint and feathered outfit, Lewis was certain was Sitting Bull, the most experienced of all the warriors. The famous war chief was looking in the opposite direction where the gunfire was coming from, and then was suddenly aware of the oncoming troopers of Reno's command behind him, and he seemed to lose all incentive to attack. Instead he began riding toward Reno and his troopers without weapons drawn, as if to talk. Others followed. But instead of receiving the gesture of surrender, Reno gave the order to open fire. Bullets struck two of Sitting Bull's warriors and they tumbled from their horses.

Lewis could only watch in shock as Sitting Bull's peaceful overture turned into a full scale attack by the soldiers, firing blindly since they were still too far apart for close up combat. Sitting Bull's horse was shot out from under him, and the man was suddenly raging with fury.

"Halt!" Reno commanded. "Prepare to fight on foot! Dismount!"

Each trooper was given a number to be used in just such a line of defense. Numbers One thru

Three leaped from their horses, giving the reins to Number Four, which was Lewis's number. He moved the horses back out of the line of fire.

The fighting men numbered about ninety and deployed themselves about five yards apart to form a skirmish line and marched ahead on foot. Each company flag bearer stabbed their flag into the ground to flutter in the breeze.

The troopers began to fire at the fast approaching warriors even though they were still just out of range. Lewis looked to Reno to see what his next command would be and saw the flask again go to his lips. Almost belatedly, Reno decided they were too exposed and needed to fall back into the timber along the river.

As the warriors bore down on them, the soldiers had no choice but to break and run. A few stayed behind to hold the Indians off until the others could reach cover.

Lewis led his horses forward for their riders, and the skirmish quickly turned into a rout. Once mounted, the troops followed Reno as he galloped thru the forest for the hills beyond.

The warriors gave chase, firing at the fleeing troops, sometimes hitting a horse or a trooper.

Lewis urged his horse through the heavy growth,

trying to stay close to cover. He'd never been this scared in the battles during the Civil War. There were terrifying stories about what Indians did to wounded enemies. Better to put a bullet in your own head then let your self be captured.

"For God's sake, don't leave me!" he heard a wounded trooper cry out.

"Hide!" Reno yelled. "We'll come back for you." They both knew that was an empty promise.

Eventually the troops reached a bastion of rocks where they could take cover and open fire on their attackers.

Once the Indians saw they had lost the advantage, they broke off the attack.

Behind his cover of rocks, Lewis collapsed to his knees with dry heaves, exhausted, thirsty, hungry, and thoroughly demoralized by Reno's actions. They'd lost too many men. Three officers and twenty-nine troopers had been killed, plus one officer and about thirteen men were missing, though some eventually found their way back.

What made Lewis's hair stand on end were the screams of the wounded soldiers being tortured and scalped, and feeling totally helpless.

One of their doctors had been killed. The remaining one was seeing to their wounded as best he could with few supplies. But now, Reno was urging them on, hoping to find Benteen or Custer. But mostly they needed water. When they came to a creek flowing between the hills, they paused to water their horses, and themselves and fill their canteens. It didn't help morale to see Reno again take out the flask.

As they again reached one of the hilltops, Lewis could see across the Little Big Horn River where there was the largest Indian village he had ever seen. Sounds of battle reached them, as they saw troopers and Indians in a fierce fire fight. The air was so thick with dust it was difficult to see how it was going, but Lewis guessed there were at least 800 warriors. They had grossly miscalculated the number of Indians in the area.

The troopers appeared to be Captain Benteen's command from the glimpse he had of the banner.

Lewis watched in horror as a number of troopers tried to make a stand at the river bottom to allow the rest of the men to escape to higher ground. It didn't take long for the massive force of Indians to ride them down.

Captain Benteen was fleeing at the head of his troops when he spotted Reno and what was left of his command, but Reno was breathing heavily, seeming oblivious to Benteen's plight.

"For God's sake, Benteen," he said. "Halt your command and help me, I've lost half my men!"

Lewis could only stare at his commander then at the play of emotions on Benteen's face. Shock. Incredulity, then apparently realizing he was dealing with a man he never liked anyway, Benteen could only ask, "Where's Custer?"

25

As the two companies went in search of Custer, whom they presumed to be somewhere up the Little Big Horn River, Lewis felt his horse stagger from exhaustion. They'd been moving constantly for three days and the troopers had not been able to carry adequate feed for their horses. And they had no way to get fresh supplies from their supply train or their supply ship the Far West which waited for them somewhere along the Big Horn River; the Little Big Horn being too narrow a flow to allow it.

They were able to water their horses again at a creek crossing, but Lewis had dropped so far back he was the last one to take advantage of the mostly muddy flow. His horse stood with its head down and clearly could go no further.

Dismounting, Lewis stroked his exhausted animal.

He wanted to yell to his comrades to let them know he wasn't following, but they were too far away. He was alone. He stripped his gear from the animal, took what he could carry and hid the saddle and bridle in the heavy undergrowth. Shuddering as if in relief, the horse began to browse on any grass it could find, and Lewis was suddenly very much alone.

Then, somewhere in the distance came the sound of rapid gunfire as another furious battle raged. He climbed up the closest hill, keeping low as he tried to pinpoint where the gunfire was coming from. It was too far away to be Reno and Benteen, and from the wrong direction.

Before long, all went quiet. It had lasted maybe thirty minutes so Lewis assumed the troopers had beaten off an Indian attack.

Feeling too exposed on the hilltop, he looked around to get his bearings. Only green rolling hills in every direction with a number of creeks and rivers winding between some of them. From the angle of the sun, he knew it was late afternoon. In vain he searched for any sign of the troops or even the pack train with their supplies so he could get a fresh horse. A light breeze cooled the sweat on his face.

His only option was to keep moving. Reno would

never send anyone to look for him, assuming he was either wounded or dead. Going back to the bottom of the arroyo, he tried to head in the direction the gunfire had come from. The Indian village would be to his left, so he needed to head northeast.

He hadn't gone far when he heard the sound of many horses above on the ridge. Heaving a vast sigh of relief Lewis spotted a long column of soldiers, riding in twos behind their commander. They moved silently, the only sound that of the horses. No conversation.

Reinforcements, Lewis thought and was about to burst from his cover to hail them, but something stopped him at the last moment. Where were the regimental colors? And the silence of the men was almost eerie.

And then he noticed holes in some of the uniforms, saw long braided hair and bows and arrows slung across the men's backs. Some horses had military style saddles, others, near the rear of the column had only blankets. In shock he gaped at Indians dressed in the uniforms of dead soldiers, riding toward the last known direction of Reno and Benteen's troops.

Somehow he had to warn them. He waited until the column of Indians was out of sight before he began to run down a parallel arroyo, heading where he thought he had heard the gunfire earlier. But it wasn't long before he realized he was totally lost. In his panic to warn his fellow troopers he suddenly had no sense of direction

When he turned into a ravine he hoped would take him to the bluff, suddenly a group of Indians materialized in front of him. They all froze, staring in shock. Lewis saw an Indian family, a man with a crippled arm, two squaws and four children, one just a baby in one woman's arms. Though his gun was still in its holster, Lewis made no move to draw it. The Indian pulled a knife, but when Lewis didn't move, they only stared at each other.

Long Bow had not returned from battle so Little Elk was doing as his brother told him, to keep their family safe. For many long minutes the Indians stared at the disheveled trooper, the two women clutching their children closer as if to shield them, eyes wide with fear. Since neither of them wanted to do battle, it was finally Little Elk who made the first move. He pointed to a branching arroyo. "Soldiers," he said.

Lewis nodded gratefully, now aware he had been headed in the wrong direction. He was too exhausted and weak to want to fight, especially against women and children.

Little Elk hesitated only a moment until he realized there was no fight left in the trooper. "Bad thing," he said, searching for English words. "Tribes leave fast. Very bad. I follow horses. Go home. Far away." Then he hurried the women on their way. He cast one look back at the exhausted trooper and something unsaid passed between them. All the fighting, the loss of life, at the moment seemed so useless.

Hunger was gnawing at him. Lewis couldn't even remember when he had eaten last. He followed the arroyo the Indian had pointed out, moving as fast as he could in his weakened condition. Then, in the distance a lone figure was climbing up a hill slowly, almost painfully. Realizing he was Indian, Lewis crouched and watched how cautiously the man was moving, as if afraid of what lay ahead. There was something familiar about him. Then he realized it was one of Custer's Crow scouts. Starting toward him, Lewis gave a low whistle he knew the man would recognize.

Curley was a warrior in his prime with a thick mane of long brownish hair, partly in braids on the sides of his dusky face, partly curly in the back. He spoke some English. At the familiar whistle he turned to see the lone trooper coming out of an arroyo and waited for him to catch up.

"What…?" Lewis started, then broke off in confusion when he saw tears on the Indian's cheeks.

Curley motioned toward the top of the hill where Lewis saw dead horses, and what looked to be numerous bodies.

"Custer?" Lewis ventured.

Curley only nodded as he continued up the hill. Lewis hurried after him, and the scene they came upon he could only describe as a soldier's worst nightmare. It was obvious that with no cover available to fight off the attacking Indians, the troopers had been forced to shoot their horses and use them for cover. Naked bodies were everywhere. Lewis lost count as he searched for any sign of life.

In the distance they heard gunfire, a steady barrage. Lewis could only guess that the columns of disguised Indians had located Captains Reno and Benteen. Helplessly he and Curley could only stand and listen. It was a short battle as little by little the gun shots faded away. A huge cloud of dust rose into the evening air on the far hill and seemed to be headed for the Indian village.

Lewis turned back to the horrendous scene in front of him. All the dead soldiers had been stripped of their uniforms, their bodies mutilated, heads scalped. It was impossible to recognize any of them. He knew then what the young Indian had meant. A very bad thing had happened, and the reaction in Washington and all across the country would forever change the future of all Indians.

Curley was standing over one particular body, wiping his eyes, and Lewis wouldn't have recognized General Custer if not for the white buckskin hat lying next to him.

Near tears himself, Lewis approached the body of the General. There were two bullet holes in his chest and one to his head. And, as he and Curly began searching among the fallen men, they found no survivors. Only a scene of total horror.

"We go," Curly urged, pointing north. "General Terry."

Lewis stumbled after him, reeling in total shock. Among the dead he had recognized the reporter from the New York Herald, Mark Kellogg; Custer's two younger brothers, Captain Tom Custer, and Boston Custer; his brother-in-law Lieutenant James Calhoun; and a nephew, seventeen year old Harry "Autie" Reed.

The supply ship the Far West, was able to moor at the head waters of the Big Horn River. And, about the time Lewis and Curley reached the ship hours later, they saw a column of soldiers coming from the south. It was obvious they had recently seen action and many were wounded.

Lewis told General Terry the news about Custer but there was little time to react as the doctors began to bark orders to receive the wounded men. They cut grass and sod from the nearby meadow to line the deck area, then covered it with tarps. It made a more than adequate field hospital.

Captain Benteen gave his report to General Terry about the Indians dressed in trooper uniforms that had almost fooled them. It was their Arikara scouts who realized they weren't soldiers but Sioux Indians. Robbed of a surprise attack, the Sioux broke off and fled back toward their village.

The moment all the wounded were aboard and undergoing treatment, Grant Marsh, Captain of the Far West was ready to pull up anchor and was calling for a full head of steam, but Terry told him to wait for his order. The remaining troops were ordered to return to their respective forts once they had off loaded their much needed supplies.

In the meantime, General Terry, who had made his headquarters aboard the Far West, called Reno and Benteen to his office where Lt. Lewis and Curley waited to give their full report.

This time, Lewis could barely hold back the tears as he described the horrors he had witnessed on that hill. He told about seeing Indians dressed as soldiers. At that point, Benteen took up the story of how they were almost fooled by them, but drove them off after only a short battle.

General Terry gave Benteen and Reno orders not to discuss the Custer disaster with any reporters, and to head back to that hill with a burial detail, to bury Custer and his men where they fell. No outsiders were to view those bodies, and they were never to speak of their mutilation.

The moment the two officers had left the ship, Terry gave orders to cast off, and make Bismarck with all possible speed so President Grant could be notified of the disaster. He kept Lt. Lewis on board as the only eye witness to the site of the disaster. Curley returned to the regiments with Reno.

Lewis, too, was forbidden to speak of the disaster with reporters on board, other than to say Custer died bravely and he and his troopers would be buried in their uniforms.

After much debate with his staff on how to write the report, Terry prepared two dispatches. One was for public distribution and made no attempt to find fault, and another was a private communication for

General Philip Sheridan that blamed the catastrophe on Custer.

Many of the wounded were in need of medical services only available at Fort Lincoln, and during the delay in casting off, the doctors did what they could to assist the injured. By the time Terry was ready to give the order to cast off, fourteen of the wounded were improved enough that they could stay at the encampment.

Lewis suspected the delay was so General Terry and his staff could come up with the wording for their dispatches. But once Terry gave the order to cast off, it was a wild ride from the narrow winding stream of the Big Horn River, to the somewhat wider Yellowstone, scraping over sand bars, bouncing off rocky banks, sometimes throwing men to the decks.

At the first opportunity, Lewis sought out a remote corner of the ship, having snatched up a sandwich and a cup of hot coffee. He was half starved. And only now did he let the tears flow freely as the images he had seen on that hill played over and over in his mind. It was a scene he would never erase.

At night it was almost impossible to see the river, but Marsh continued to push his steamer for every ounce of speed he could. Usually a ship would tie up at night rather than risk ship and crew in the dark, but this was no ordinary run.

The Far West made all possible speed as it traveled from the Yellowstone to the Missouri River, with her iron chimneys belching out twin trails of soot and ash. Breaking all speed records, they reached Bismarck about 11 p.m. There, they woke the telegraph operator who sent the messages of the Custer disaster to President Grant and to General Sheridan. For the rest of the night the operator was kept busy sending reports of the biggest story of the Indian wars to newspapers across the country.

Of the Seventh Cavalry's approximately 750 officers and enlisted men, 268 had been killed, losing not only their leader but almost half of their officers and men, one of the most devastating losses in the history of the Indian Wars.

26

John Jay hadn't been asleep long that night when Abby suddenly leaped out of bed, crying "No! No!"

He went to her side but she pushed him away. At first, he thought something in the bed had bitten her, until he saw her attention was directed inward. "No!" she cried again. "Stupid! Stupid!" She broke down in tears, sitting down abruptly on the bed. This time she allowed John Jay to hold her in his arms.

"So stupid!" she moaned again.

"What's happened?" he asked, wanting to understand her terror.

"All dead," she whispered. "Soldiers, fighting Indians."

"Kumeyaay?"

"No, not our people. Others. Sioux, I think,

and they're all dead."

"The Indians?" He was struggling to make sense of her words.

"No, the soldiers. All the soldiers," she whispered. "The Indians made certain there were no survivors."

For several minutes John Jay rocked her as she slowly calmed.

"We have to leave," she said, still partly in the grip of the vision that had awakened her.

"What?"

"Word will come for us to leave. Now. Tonight! Tomorrow at the latest. We must get ready."

John Jay didn't question her vision. With others of the family now returned to their own homes, only Malinda and her helpers remained. They didn't wake the household or the children as they began to pack up all their belongings. But the activity woke the others and food was prepared for the journey.

Daniel woke to a pounding on his front door. Getting out of bed he went to the window and opened it. In front of his house was one man on horseback holding the reins of two other horses. A second man was out of sight on the porch, pounding on his door. He recognized the man on the horse as one of President Grant's security guards and former soldier, Robert Lewis.

"Lewis, what's up?" he called down.

The pounding stopped, the second man stepped out to where he could see Daniel. "The President wants you. Now! Plan to be gone several days," Alfred Jenner called up to him.

Daniel realized that he'd be riding the third horse so he scrambled into riding clothes and packed a satchel with toiletries and underwear.

"What's happened?" Julia asked sleepily.

"I don't know. Something drastic for Grant to send for me in the middle of the night." Leaning down he planted a quick kiss on her lips. "I'll try to let you know what's going on…but I may not be back for a couple of days."

Julia knew better than to ask questions when there were no answers to be had. "Be safe," she whispered and held him in a quick embrace.

"I love you," he called as he headed out the door.

The men wasted no time with words as they rode out of the yard and through the dark streets of D.C. on their way to the White House.

Daniel knew these men wouldn't have been told what the crises was. And, as for himself, as Assistant Treasurer, he couldn't think of any situation that would call for his presence in the middle of the night. It must relate to the Indian situation in California, but even then, what could be so urgent?

When they reined in at the private side entrance to the White House, Daniel saw one of the President's coaches pulling up on standby. His two escorts took him as far as the President's office, announced him, and then closed the door behind them.

Daniel was startled by President Grant's appearance. Where he had always been neatly dressed and well groomed, tonight his hair was uncombed, he was unshaven, his clothing rumpled and he was pacing nervously.

Two small desks had been brought in and two of his male clerks were busy copying documents for the President's signature.

"Daniel, thank God you're here!" Grant said, grabbing his hand and pumping it.

"What's happened, Mister President?"

"Custer! That...that idiot has gone and gotten himself and his entire command wiped out. Not one single survivor. Chief Crazy Horse saw to that!"

The news hit Daniel like a rock. His knees gave way as he sank to his haunches. "All…dead?" he questioned in disbelief. He'd met Custer a number of times, and knew his reputation as a tough fighting man in spite of all his grandstanding. "How?"

Grant shrugged his shoulders. "God only knows, but he's always underestimated the Indians. This is a horrendous disaster."

Daniel slowly got to his feet looking puzzled. "But, why am I here?"

"Today we finally worked out reservations for nine of the areas in San Diego County. I've been up all night finalizing them, and my clerks are making the copies they will need in California. One for Sacramento, one for the San Diego County Indian Commissioner, and one for each reservation."

"…But…why so urgent?"

"If we wait until tomorrow when my cabinet meets and gets the news about Custer, they'll call all these back, and we'll be back where we were on day one." Grant was pacing nervously. "I need you to take these to Abby and John Jay. I've already sent them a telegram to be in Syracuse ready to board the Cross Country Express. You'll meet them there with the proclamations."

"How?" Daniel was struggling to understand.

"The carriage outside will take you to the train station where my car is waiting with one engine. It will take you to New York City to board the Express. They've been instructed not to leave without you. And they've been instructed not to leave Syracuse without the Butterfields. You get off there and make your way back here any way you can." Grant barely paused for breath. "Lewis will go with you so he can report back to me along the way."

The moment the documents were completed by his sleepy-eyed clerks, President Grant signed them, stamped them with his official seal and placed them into a sturdy satchel.

"Safe journey," Grant called as Daniel grabbed the satchel and headed out to the carriage where Robert Lewis joined him. Now he could tell his escort the terrible news.

The carriage drove through the dark streets of D.C. to the train station. Daniel had never seen the President's private car, and was deeply honored to be given its use. There were plush furnishings, a bedroom, and a kitchen where the President's personal porter was there to wait on them.

Too upset by the terrible news to rest, Daniel and Lewis both ordered breakfast as the train traveled at top speed. The tracks ahead of them had been hurriedly cleared. Hopefully they'd make it to New York City and the Express Train Station at close to its usual departure time.

To pass the time, they found a deck of cards. Both men had known General George Custer, and thought him cocky. He'd wanted to make a name for himself by settling the Sioux and Cheyenne Indian problems once and for all, but he had grossly underestimated Chief Crazy Horse and Chief Sitting Bull. It was bad enough that Custer was killed, but his entire command who had no choice but to follow him into battle had perished with him.

Daniel could well imagine what the reaction would be later in the morning in D.C. when the news reached the President's Cabinet and Congress. All Indians were going to feel the fury of the white man's government, and Grant wouldn't be able to control it...which is why he had acted so swiftly to send Daniel on this mission with the legal reservation grants before they could be recalled.

"So Lewis," John Jay said as he dealt the cards. "This is the first chance we've had to talk. How do you like working for President Grant?"

Lewis looked his cards over, shifted several of them and discarded two. "It makes me feel useful now that the war is over. I saw a lot of action. Was under Grant's command most of the time, so I'm glad I can still serve him."

"Any trouble come with the job?"

"Not really. There's also an outer ring of security that usually catches the disgruntled Southerners. Mostly Jenner and I deal with the inner circle of his Cabinet and Congress."

Daniel discarded one card then picked up the deck to deal Lewis two cards and himself one.

"What about your nephew, David? Last I heard he'd enlisted shortly before the end of the war."

Lewis moved the two new cards into his hand and scowled at the results.

"Yeah, last I heard he was with Custer."

Daniel stared at Lewis with a big question in his eyes. One he was afraid to voice.

"I don't know," Lewis said in a shaky voice. "Other than Custer, we have no names of the other casualties. I didn't even know about Custer until you told me."

"Has there been a lot of trouble with the Indians?"

"Oh yeah. The army is trying to keep the warriors contained to reservations. But if they have a hankering to hunt buffalo or visit another village, they just go. It was driving Custer crazy. We've heard rumors about some major operation coming up. Crook, Gibbons, Terry and Custer were all out there planning some big offensive."

"I'm sorry to hear that," Daniel said, losing interest in his cards. "I think the Indians are always going to get the short end of the stick."

"You should hear the stories about Crazy Horse and Sitting Bull. They refuse to be sent to a reservation." Lewis scowled at his cards then laid them down, discouraged. "I hear your brother's wife was captured by Indians as a young girl."

"Then you heard wrong. The Kumeyaay Indians found her after she'd buried her parents. Their wagon train was attacked by Apache. Except for some women and children who were carried off, she was the only survivor. The Kumeyaay found her and took her in."

"She ever try to run away?"

"There was no need. She stayed with them by choice, became a medicine woman, and eventually married James Cassidy, a station master for the Butterfield Mail. That's where my brother met her."

"I have to admit I was surprised when I saw her. She's a striking looking woman with those unusual white streaks in her hair."

"She said that happened when she met one of the ancient spirits of the Kumeyaay during her medicine woman training."

"You believe that?" Lewis asked skeptically.

"I have to. I've seen her do some amazing things, and the Indians respect her. That's the most important thing. And she's trying to help them keep their land."

"Yeah, I have mixed feelings about that. If I were Indian, I know I would resent the whites taking my land and killing off the buffalo."

"And as the Indians are being killed or forced into reservations, the white people are spouting Manifest Destiny. It is our right, they say."

"A bunch of bull!" Lewis exclaimed. "But I worry about David out there. Recruits are trained in warfare against enemies who have similar training. But Indians don't fight that way."

"No, and now, more of them have guns, which makes them even more formidable."

Lewis shook his head at the thought. "One minute I wish I was out there in the wilderness, the smell of the cook fire, nothing but prairie in every direction, and then the smell of gunpowder, the sweat, with a strong horse under you…"

"Once a soldier…" Daniel said.

"Yeah," he said in disgust. "Your stomach one big knot of fear, sweat in your eyes and a prayer on your lips…that the enemy's bullet won't find you or your horse."

Daniel looked up when the porter came in and asked for a bottle of whiskey. It soon appeared with two glasses. Daniel poured and the two men lapsed into silence, their card game forgotten. But it was clear something else was on Lewis's mind.

"You know," he said thoughtfully. "I didn't think anything about it at the time, but just before we headed for the train, my partner, Jenner, disappeared. We've worked together ever since the President took office…but Jenner hates Indians. Some of his family members were killed by them many years ago. He must have heard the news about Custer somehow and it probably hit him hard."

"Think he'd try to make trouble?"

"I hate to think it, but it's possible. Grant was sending a couple of men to his residence to try to find him. At the time, I didn't know why."

"Damn!" Daniel muttered. "What next?"

The men lapsed into silence, sipping their whiskey.

Abby, John Jay and Delfina stood on the train

platform with the children, listening to the sound of the approaching train. Delfina held four-year-old Jay who was asleep against her shoulder, while John Jay rocked a sleepy Ellie in his arms. Hours earlier the telegram reached them ordering them to meet Daniel here in Syracuse and be prepared to return to California immediately with the Presidential orders for at least some of the pending reservations. The Express train would reach San Francisco in about four days. And a steamship would be waiting to carry them to San Diego. Abby and John Jay were silent, weary from the abrupt leave-taking of John Jay's mother, knowing it would be a long time before they saw her again. Delfina stood silent, stoic. She'd seen many amazing things on this trip for an Indian woman raised in a remote village. But she'd worked in a few white households before the Butterfields...and couldn't wait to tell the stories to her grandchildren.

She also understood that the massacre of General Custer and his men would be a bad thing for all Indians...understood that the President had acted for the California Indians before he could be stopped once the news spread.

For all of them, it was almost a feeling of having to sneak out of town.

Daniel was already standing on the outside steps of the passenger car reserved for the Butterfield party. As the train stopped, he gave his brother a hug, and Abby, then took little Jay from Delfina's arms and kissed him before setting him on his feet. Jay stared wide eyed at the huge train, aware it had made a special stop just for them. Daniel then told them the details that the telegram couldn't, about the crises with General Custer.

"The satchel is on board, all signed for the Indian Commissioner and each reservation. The governor will receive his copy by a separate courier," Daniel told them. "Safe trip, brother. Keep in touch."

"Thanks Daniel. You've had one heck of a night."

"That I have. But I'd love to be in Washington right now, to hear the reaction to the President's actions."

"The People will be forever grateful," Abby said. "Even nine reservations is better than nothing."

"And it would have been nothing once the Custer news hit the President's Cabinet."

A Porter hustled the Butterfields aboard and they could only wave to Daniel as the train pulled out of the station.

Exhausted, Abby, John Jay and Delfina settled the children down to rest. Then they too settled into the plush first class seats, exhausted.

Daniel stood alone on the train platform, his own satchel at his feet as he watched the Express disappear. Lewis had returned to Washington in the President's car when Daniel had boarded the waiting Express. And now, Daniel was a long way from home. His first duty was to go into the station to send a telegram to President Grant that all had gone according to plan, and that the Butterfields and the Presidential orders were on their way to California.

Free now of any immediate duties, he walked to the local train station to wait for the next departure for Utica. He'd spend the night at his mother's and return to Washington the following day.

27

General Custer's 7th Cavalry of about two hundred and ten troopers had been wiped out. Fortunately though the entire Cavalry was not destroyed. Major Marcus Reno and Captain Frederick Benteen, commanding about four hundred troopers and scouts all managed to survive.

In Washington DC, there was a great deal of fallout from the massacre of Custer's command. Accusations were made of orders disobeyed by Major Reno and Captain Benteen. Custer was criticized for his tactics, but with so much conflicting testimony, no firm conclusions could be reached.

President Grant had been right about one thing. The reaction of both Congress and the public was an outcry against all Indians. More troops were mobilized with the goal of permanently forcing all Indians onto reservations.

Grant's cabinet demanded to review those California reservations they had previously approved, only to learn it was too late. The records were on their way to California.

Congress responded by issuing the Indian Appropriations Act of 1876, to cut off any rations for the Sioux until they ended hostilities and ceded the Black Hills to the government. This officially took away the Sioux land, and established reservations for them, partly due to the fact that gold had been discovered in the Black Hills.

Security Guard Lewis learned of his nephew's survival of the Indian battles, and that he was on his way to Washington with General Terry as the only eyewitness to the scene of the massacre.

But what troubled Robert Lewis was the fact that his usual partner in guarding the President's office had disappeared. When Grant's men went to his home, they found it deserted, abruptly, and now Lewis was afraid of what that meant. Daniel needed to notify the Butterfields to be on their guard.

28

O nce the train was moving, Abby and John Jay could finally relax. Ellie and Jay had their faces glued to the windows watching in fascination as they moved through New York, then out into a land of scattered homes and farms.

The Porter served them a snack of miniature sandwiches, fruit, and iced tea for the adults, juice for the children.

Delfina, too, was fascinated by the countryside, and, inside her, the knowledge that once this land had belonged to various indigenous tribes, now displaced by a force they were trying desperately to stop. But, inside her, too, was the knowledge she was helping Eagle Woman as she fought the overwhelming tide of Whites, trying to save land for her people. And here, with them, was a satchel with the Presidential orders that gave Indians their own land. She knew it was something the three of them would defend with their lives if necessary.

She had seen John Jay hide the satchel under some seats near the front of their private coach, where they could always keep an eye on it. And, often, she would look to make certain it was still there. There were only two cars behind them, a mail car and one for railroad personnel. There would be no strangers venturing into their car. Plus, she glimpsed guards in the cars on either side of them to protect their privacy.

Abby, too, was fascinated by the ever changing countryside, but she was weary from the abrupt leave taking of John Jay's family. Now they could relax and turn their seats into beds, their Porter providing pillows and blankets.

Soon the children, too, were ready to nap, and the Express Train moved steadily through the countryside, the blast of the whistle sounding distant with the steam engine so many cars away.

Four days later, when the train pulled into San Francisco, two military men came aboard to help them move their belongings to a waiting carriage.

John Jay took control of the precious satchel, refusing to let anyone else handle it. The two soldiers escorted them to the harbor where the mail ship, the *SS California*, was waiting for them, and for any other mail also being shuttled from the Express to the ship.

Little effort was required by Abby and family. President Grant had made all the arrangements, so they were treated like royalty.

On the *California* they were given adjoining cabins, one for Abby and John Jay, the other for Delfina and the children. A personal maid was assigned to assist Delfina.

The *SS California* was a mail ship that traveled from Oregon, and down the coast of California, stopping at major cities along the way. After San Francisco, were Monterey, Los Angeles and San Diego. Then it continued to Panama where the mail was transferred to a train that crossed the isthmus to the Gulf of Mexico where another steam ship carried the mail to various ports along the way to New York City.

In addition to being a mail ship, the *California* also had several cabins for travelers to help pay for the mail service, though it couldn't offer the amenities of a large passenger ship. There was a dining room with a kitchen staff providing good meals, without the extra exotic offerings of a big ship. But there were rarely complaints. The food was nourishing and plentiful. The crew ate the same food as the passengers, though in their own dining room.

One of the first things John Jay and Abby did, still in the company of their military escort, was to ask the Captain to lock the precious satchel in his safe. He was expecting the request after receiving a telegram from President Grant himself.

The first evening at sea, Abby and John Jay went to the dining room for supper. Delfina and the children chose to be served in their cabin, with the help of the maid.

"Marta is so good with the children," Abby remarked as they relaxed with a glass of wine, waiting for their food. "We won't have to worry about them."

"The President certainly cleared the way for us. I've never had such an easy trip," John Jay agreed.

As she looked around the dining room, Abby saw a number of other passengers having dinner. Her gaze settled on two men at a table on the far side of the room. One man was looking directly at her but looked away quickly.

For a moment Abby studied the two. They were dressed in rough clothing, more like working men than passengers. Yet, she knew they weren't crew or they'd be eating elsewhere. She made a quick mental note of them, then turned her attention to the arrival of their food.

John Jay saw her slight frown. "Something wrong?"

"Those two men by the side door."

Trying not to be obvious, John Jay glanced their way just in time to see their backs as they went out the door. "What about them?"

"I'm not sure. One of them looked away so quickly when our eyes met…like he didn't want me to know…" she shrugged, unable to put it into words.

John Jay knew better than to discount her feelings. "We'll keep an eye out for them."

After dinner, as they were headed back to their cabin, Abby tapped lightly on the door to the children's room. Marta opened the door, but frowned when she saw they were in their evening clothes.

"Something wrong, Marta?" Abby asked.

"Well…I heard you come back earlier so I knocked on your door." She hesitated. "When you didn't answer, I thought maybe…" she was blushing. "You didn't want to be disturbed."

John Jay's hand went immediately to the small pistol in his coat pocket. "Keep the door closed," he ordered Marta as he headed for their room, handing Abby the key. She unlocked their door then stood back as John Jay silently opened the door.

Only one lamp partially lit the room...but it was obvious the room was empty. Abby followed him inside. It was also obvious the room had been searched. Abby saw her medicine satchel standing open with some items dumped on the floor. They knew what the men had been searching for.

Abby went back to the children's room to let Delfina and Marta know everything was okay.

"What should I have done?" Marta wailed, shaken, as if it were all her fault.

"Exactly what you did," Abby told her. "Nothing. These men can be dangerous."

John Jay headed for the control room to talk to the Captain when he felt the ship shudder as it bumped a pier. Knowing the next stop was Monterey, he ran for the gangplank where a few passengers and mail were disembarking. Only a few lamps lit the wharf, but he was in time to see two men disappearing into the night.

One of them stopped to look back, startled to see John Jay watching them, but too far away to pose a danger. Then they were gone.

Unsure what to do, John Jay watched the spot where the men had been. He couldn't leave the ship. The stop was only long enough to off load the mail and passengers and take on any new mail…no more than thirty minutes. Notifying the local sheriff seemed useless.

He was aware of Abby coming to his side. "Gone?" she asked.

He nodded. "They didn't find what they wanted. I find it hard to believe they could be after the President's orders so soon."

"Someone obviously sent word," Abby said with a worried frown. "Once we reach San Diego we will need an armed escort."

There was no way to send a telegram from the ship, but it was obvious, as the *California* pulled up to the pier in San Diego, President Grant had foreseen the need. An escort of four soldiers and one Captain were waiting for them.

It was not yet daylight when Abby, John Jay, Delfina and the children bid farewell to their maid, Marta, and the ship's Captain, and boarded a carriage that took them to a nearby hotel. John Jay had retrieved the satchel from the Captain's safe and, with armed guards stationed at both of their rooms, John Jay elected to keep the satchel with them in their room. The hotel safe was too small to hold it.

"I can't believe this," Abby said. "How could

word have traveled so fast?"

"Well, the President could do it, to have us met all along the way. Obviously someone else made similar contact with someone to stop this satchel from ever reaching the Commissioner."

A knock at the door startled them. There were guards at the door so it was likely one of them, but to be safe, John Jay stood out of sight, pistol in his hand.

Abby opened the door to find one of the soldiers holding a telegram.

"Message, ma'am," he said, handing it to her.

"Thank you," she said, closed and locked the door. She handed the telegram to John Jay since it was addressed to him.

"From Daniel," he said. "The missing security guard disappeared. His room cleared. Hates Indians. Watch your back."

"He must have contacts," Abby said. "And he might not be far behind us."

"We can't let these records out of our sight," John Jay said. He went to the door to see the two soldiers posted in the hall. Others would be posted downstairs.

"Would you tell Captain Moreno I'd like to see him," John Jay said to them.

"Yes, sir," one of them replied. "He's downstairs."

The soldier left. John Jay closed and locked the door until a knock came about twenty minutes later.

"Thank you for coming, Captain Moreno, I just received this telegram from my brother, who is a member of the President's team," He waited while Jenkins read the message. "The Security guard went missing right after the news of General Custer's massacre, and is a known Indian hater after losing his family when he was a boy. He was the only survivor, so he saw what they did to his parents and brothers and sisters. He knew the President rushed these records through that are in this satchel. And we believe he wants to stop the confirmation of these reservations…or at the very least, delay them. We've already had one attempt aboard the *California*."

"So you think they'll make another attempt to stop you from reaching the Commissioner?" Moreno asked. To John Jay he looked skeptical.

"I think we can count on it."

"Okay. We'll keep our eyes open."

The Captain left to confer with his men, telling them to be extra alert. They had about three hours before the Commissioner would be in his office.

Abby used the pitcher of water to freshen up. Weary, but too keyed up to sleep. She could only hope Captain Moreno took the threat seriously.

John Jay pulled off his boots and lay on the bed to rest. They hadn't had much sleep after the incident on the ship.

Sitting at the dressing table, Abby pulled the pins from the bun she wore her hair in, the light from the lamp reflecting off the two white wings at her temples. She leaned closer, still amazed by them, and how they had appeared when she and Enyaa, her medicine teacher, had visited the sacred cave. She'd had a vision that seemed so real. She was a golden eagle, her wings streaming fire as she rose upwards toward the sun. Yet there was no sensation of heat. She had touched the sun, then abruptly awoke back in the cave.

The spirits had accepted her and from then on, the Kumeyaay called her Eagle Woman.

Just thinking about her wings of flame, Abby imagined she could smell smoke. But the scent was strong. John Jay, too, sat up and pulled on his boots as a pounding came at the door. He opened it to find a soldier looking scared.

"There's a fire, Mr. Butterfield. It's the stairs. We

can't go down that way. My men are waking the other guests, there's only two other rooms occupied."

Abby joined John Jay and looked toward the stairwell where smoke and flames were visible. It was the only way out, except for windows.

Delfina opened the door to the children's room to see what the shouting was about.

"Abby," John Jay said, "You get the children and their things ready." He looked at the soldier. "We'll go out their window. You go open that one while I gather up our things."

Two soldiers were assisting the other guests in going out their windows to safety. In the streets there was shouting as a fire brigade assembled to fight the flames.

John Jay opened the window in their room and tossed their luggage to soldiers below, and more men were gathering. He kept only Abby's medicine bag and the satchel containing the reservation records.

He went back to the children's room just in time to see Jay trustingly leap from the window into the arms of a soldier below.

Ellie was screaming in fear, so Delfina went out next, another soldier breaking her fall and setting her on her feet.

Abby tried to soothe Ellie as John Jay closed the door to the hall against the smoke and flames inching closer.

The soldier with them stood by to help any way he could, but he, too, looked scared.

Abby carried Ellie to the window. Below them, a flatbed wagon had been pulled up to shorten the distance to the ground. Two soldiers lifted Delfina onto the wagon and she reached up her arms for Ellie.

"Hush now, sweetheart," Abby soothed her. "Delfina won't let you fall."

Without giving the girl time to think, Abby thrust her out the open window and dropped her into Delfina's waiting arms. The two were quickly lifted down to safety.

John Jay turned to the soldier. "You go next…"

"No! I go last!" he insisted.

"Listen! This satchel contains Presidential orders. I think it's why the fire was set. I'll drop this to you and you guard it with your life. Understand?"

"Yes, sir." The soldier fit himself out onto an outer edge of the window. Two more soldiers stood on the wagon to help break his fall, then when he was safely down, he turned to catch the satchel.

Abby had been watching the scene below, and

quickly began to throw the children's luggage down, watching the reaction of the bystanders.

"Don't!" she said when John Jay started to take the satchel.

"Abby, what…?"

Instead she thrust her medicine bag down. A trooper caught it, went to set it with the rest of their things when suddenly a group of four men broke their way through the soldiers whose attention was on the window. One of them grabbed Abby's satchel then they turned and ran.

"Halt!" "Stop!" the soldiers shouted and gave chase.

John Jay saw then that Abby had suspected the ploy, and by now the remaining soldiers formed a ring, facing outward to prevent further theft. John Jay then dropped the Presidential satchel to the soldier on the wagon. With it safely at his feet, the man then reached up for Abby as she jumped, aiming her hands for his shoulders. He caught her around the waist and set her gently on her feet next to him. She scrambled down from the wagon, taking the satchel with her. And was quickly ringed by soldiers. John Jay dropped onto the wagon.

The fire brigade was running in and out of the

front door of the hotel, throwing buckets of water on the flames.

"What about the other guests?" John Jay asked.

"They're safe," a soldier said. "No one was hurt, just a lot of damage to the stairs and part of the hall."

"Good. We need a carriage."

"On its way."

"Over here!" a soldier called from an alleyway.

Abby stayed with the satchel while John Jay went to where the soldier was standing over some scattered items on the ground. Next to them was Abby's medicine bag. He was grinning as he gathered the items.

"They'll be back," John Jay predicted.

Now the soldiers took him seriously, and more men in uniform joined the protective brigade.

Abby was happy to have her bag back, only slightly worse for wear. She took Ellie from Delfina as a carriage pulled up in the street for them. John Jay tossed the satchel in first, Delfina climbed in next and Abby handed Ellie to her. John Jay lifted his son in, Abby followed, and, after a last look around at the large escort surrounding the carriage, he climbed in and closed the door...waiting while the soldiers loaded the rest of their luggage into the rear boot.

"I wanna be a soldier when I grow up," Jay announced. "They're brave. They saved us."

"Yes, they did," John Jay agreed.

"So-jer!" Ellie exclaimed.

"Yes, sweetheart," Abby said. "So-jers!" She looked at Delfina who seemed unfazed by events.

"Thank you, grandmother. You are a blessing to the children and me."

"They are like my own," she said, dismissing her part in the escape from the fire. "Those bad men, they be back."

"Yes, I'm sure you're right."

With the excitement over, Ellie curled up on Delfina's lap ready to nap again. But Jay was too excited and watched out the window to see where they were going and wave to their soldier escort.

In the downtown area of San Diego they pulled up in front of a large office building with barred windows. Abby had been here before. The Commissioner's office.

The carriage with their luggage waited outside. The only thing Abby and John Jay took inside was the President's satchel.

"Mrs. Butterfield!" the Commissioner greeted her, taking her hand. "What a terrible experience you've had!" He looked at John Jay. "And you must be her husband, John Jay Butterfield. It's an honor to meet you, sir."

"Thank you, Commissioner," John Jay said. "I can't tell you how relieved we are to deliver this satchel to you."

"Please, sit, sit," he said motioning them to a sofa against one wall. He took an overstuffed chair facing them. Delfina and the children found a play area near a large stone fireplace. "I've ordered breakfast for all of us, since none of us have had a chance to eat."

He was eying the satchel sitting on the floor by John Jay's feet with curiosity.

"That will be most welcome," Abby said. "And I hope you have a very secure place for this."

"Oh, yes. You have made excellent time bringing that clear from Washington D.C. in less than a week. We heard what happened to General Custer. A terrible tragedy."

"Yes," John Jay agreed. "The President was afraid these nine reservations would be rescinded, so he hurried the records through to get them out of town."

"Once I heard from President Grant that these were on their way, I contacted Captain Oatman who is in charge of Camp Wright and sent them to evict some squatters the surveyors report mentioned," the Commissioner said. "Some of them were living in little more than hovels."

"Yes," Abby agreed. "I saw some of them when we did the surveying."

"So how do we present these to the clans involved?"

"I'm thinking a big gathering of the nine clans. A fiesta, with you there to ceremoniously present the official record to each of the clan elders," Abby said. "Not only that, a large gathering will discourage any more attempts to steal these records, though I know your original records will remain here. The Governor will also receive copies."

"Ummm, I like that idea. A fiesta. Will you arrange that?"

"I will be happy to do that. Probably not for a month or more," Abby said. "I'd like to think there won't be any more attempts to steal these records, with a copy in Sacramento and one to remain here with you. But these men seem determined to at least delay things, if not stop them altogether."

For a moment the Commissioner was silent. "Well someone has gone to a lot of trouble tracking you across country, even going so far as to set fire to your hotel. I'm thinking we haven't seen the last of them."

John Jay scratched his two-day-old beard as his gaze first met Abbys then the Commissioners. "I hope you are wrong, but you need to guard this satchel as if it were filled with gold…just in case they're still determined to stop us."

"We think one of them is coming from Washington," Abby said. "He abandoned his post as one of President Grant's closest security men. And he supposedly hates Indians." She paused when a side door opened and a table covered with food was wheeled in.

The Commissioner dismissed the waiters so they could serve themselves. But first they had Delfina take food for the children and return to their place across the room. Then Abby and John Jay were invited to serve themselves, the Commissioner waiting until last. The aroma of fresh, hot coffee filled the room.

Once settled at the table with their food in front of them, the Commissioner looked at Abby. "You don't think he'll give up, do you?"

"He can't go back to Washington. He's risked too much. My guess is he'll first look your situation over to see if he can get close to the records."

John Jay spoke up. "If they set fire to the hotel, there's no telling what else they'll do."

For a time they were occupied with plates of scrambled eggs, bacon, biscuits and gravy, and fresh fruit. And a rich coffee and cream to go with it.

"Today we'll move to our house here in town," John Jay said. "We notified our friends, the Champions, to let them know we'll be staying at least a few days before going to the ranch."

"Once we get home," Abby said. "We can consult with the tribal elders to set a date for a fiesta."

"Any idea where it would be held?"

"About the only place that could hold a gathering of that size is a place called Campo. It's on the trail between here and Yuma Crossing."

"I know the place," the Commissioner said. "In the meantime, I'll have a large tent made for the presentations, and some others to house my staff and me."

"The tribes will be honored," Abby said. "This is a very big thing to them after years of empty promises. The celebration will go on for days."

"I have a secure safe here to hold the satchel until then."

Abby leaned toward the Commissioner. "Maybe we could do something to draw these men out.

Otherwise, once you're on the trail to Campo, even with a full contingent of military to protect you, you could still be vulnerable."

"Like what?" he asked.

"Find a similar satchel to this one and fill it with any official looking records you can afford to lose…we want these men to think they're the real ones."

The Commissioner's frown said he was already contemplating what he could use that would resemble Presidential orders. "I can arrange that. Then what?"

"Then we set a pretend date for you to travel out to Indian Country, and also pretend to keep it secret. But here and there it could be leaked…in a local saloon, at the outfitters. Only a few of your most trusted men can know the truth."

"I like that!" John Jay exclaimed, looking excited about the plan. "The group sets out with the fake records under guard. But somehow they just might manage to get stolen."

"Hopefully it won't be a violent attack," the Commissioner said.

"So far they've avoided that," John Jay said. "Maybe one of the men we suspect could accidently be hired to help with the supplies. You'll have to be hiring some locals for that…and they're going to be watching, waiting for another chance."

The plans were made, the Presidential orders locked away in a large safe in the basement. They set a date for two weeks away for the fake trek. Then a very weary Butterfield family was taken to their house not far from Old Town. Already the Champions had sent a crew to their house to put it in order, bring in supplies and leave horses and a carriage in the stable.

Andres was one of the workers, smiling at Abby when they came into the nearly clean house. Judge Hartnell knew Abby and John Jay would find him helpful.

"I was hoping to see you," she told him. "Can you get word to Night Wolf? I need to speak with him and arrange a surprise party for some men who are trying to steal the reservation records."

Andres grinned at the thought of there being some action. "I will speak to Senor Hartnell and arrange to leave this evening."

"Good. How are your wife and the baby?"

"Not a baby any more. He talks our ears off. Is learning to ride and can almost do my job better than me."

Abby laughed. "I am happy to hear that."

He was suddenly serious, "I would not be enjoying this time with my wife or my son if not for Eagle Woman."

"I'm just glad I was here when I was needed. Give them an extra hug from me."

"Gladly."

29

To Abby it felt good to have her own home again, just for her and her family, and at least two weeks before the pretend trek into the mountains.

Andres left the same evening after talking to his employers, the Hartnells. They knew if Abby requested it, it was important. His mission was twofold, to spread word among the clans that the Presidential orders had arrived, and for them to set a date for the presentation and celebration.

But Abby also requested that Night Wolf...she could never bring herself to think of him by his new Spanish name...bring half a dozen men to help set a trap for those who would sabotage the records. But they must meet secretly once they reached San Diego. She also suggested that warrior dress might scare the thieves.

When Night Wolf heard the plan, he understood. A group of warriors in buckskin loin cloths, bare chests and long straight hair would look far more fearsome than men in long pants and shirts.

Though he wasn't certain what to expect, they would take bows and arrows and lances as well as rifles and pistols. Mandy stood outside their cabin, watching the warriors preparing food and weapons for what might be days in the wilderness. Her hand went automatically to her expanding stomach which was showing signs of her advanced pregnancy.

"Tell Cousin Abby hello," she said to her tall handsome husband. "I miss her, and I'm hoping she'll be here for my baby's arrival."

"I will tell her," he said as he mounted his spirited pinto. She waved as the men rode out together.

As they neared San Diego, Andres rode on to the Champion's home while the others stayed hidden in the heavy growth along the San Diego River.

It was their fourth day at the house. Abby was in the kitchen preparing a big dinner for the family. A large pot of beans was cooking on the stove and she was using the meat grinder on last night's roast to make tamales.

John Jay was with Charles Champion fishing out near the mouth of the San Diego River, and Delfina was in the back yard with the children.

John Jay had made a swing for Jay, and a saw horse with a small saddle. For Ellie there was a sand box with some hand carved animals. So they often spent time outside playing.

Though Abby was thankful for the peace and quiet, she knew it was about time for Night Wolf and his friends to arrive. But for now, the only sound was the laughter of the children.

Her plan was to use the warriors to shadow her and the Commissioner with their small party of soldiers when they headed out with the fake papers in an attempt to draw out the thieves. If the plan was successful, Night Wolf and his warriors would be there to track them.

From outside Abby heard Delfina shouting, and Ellie screaming. She ran to the back door just as Delfina came huffing and puffing, Ellie wrapped tightly in her arms. Delfina was speaking so fast in the Kumeyaay language Abby could barely understand her. The only words that registered were "Jay" and "gone".

Abby grabbed the rifle that hung over the back door and ran outside, Delfina still jabbering frantically behind her.

The back yard was empty. "Bad men! Bad men! Take Jay!" Delfina wailed.

Abby ran to the back fence threw open the gate and stepped out into the alley, rifle held at the ready…but all was quiet. No sound of Jay's voice, no horses or wagon. Just silence except for Ellie's crying and Delfina's huffing and puffing. She had to force herself to calm down, to think what to do, who to call, when she noticed a paper nailed to the gate. Her hands were shaking as she set the rifle down and grabbed the note.

"Your son is safe." it said. "He won't be harmed unless you fail to meet our demands. You are to go to the Commissioner's office first thing tomorrow morning, alone, and get the President's satchel with the reservation records. Do not contact any authorities. We will be watching. Bring the satchel here and we will send further instructions. I don't think I have to tell you that if you ever want to see your son again you will do exactly as I say."

Abby could only hope the kidnappers would keep their word.

"It's okay," she told Delfina. "He won't be

harmed." She picked up her rifle, closed the gate and headed back for the house.

"I should have…" Delfina wailed.

"No, there was nothing you could have done," Abby soothed her, trying to keep her own heart from hammering. "We have no choice but to give them what they want."

It was then Abby remembered the fake records the Commissioner was going to prepare. Did she dare try to fool the men who had her son?

When John Jay came home with a line of fresh fish, Abby asked Charles Champion to come inside for refreshments, she said, in case anyone was listening. Delfina brought them tea, then she took the string of fish to clean and prepare to go with their dinner.

"What's wrong?" John Jay asked seeing how pale Abby was.

Charles, too, sensed something was very wrong.

"Jay has been kidnapped." She held up the note the kidnappers had left. John Jay snatched it from her hand and read it out loud.

"Have you notified the sheriff?" Charles asked.

"We can't do that," John Jay said, looking up from the note, his face also going pale. "They're very clear about that."

"Then what can we do?" Charles asked, feeling the need to do something, and suddenly wondering why Abby had chosen to share this information with him, which the note forbade.

John Jay, too, looked at Abby, knowing she had a plan. She looked at Charles. "I want you to go home as if nothing has happened. Act like you know nothing about this. Tell no one. No one!" Abby stressed. "Except Andres. Go by Judge Hartnell's to tell him to get word to Night Wolf, who should be here in the area by now. He and his warriors are the only ones who have a chance of going undetected."

For a moment she was silent, to let both her husband and Charles digest that. "Tomorrow I will go to Commissioner Higby's office and get the satchel." Her steady look at John Jay told him not to remark about the fake records. "And we will follow all instructions."

"I'll go with you," John Jay said.

"The note says I am to go alone. We must follow their directions," she told him. "I'm in no danger. So far they haven't injured anyone, in spite of the hotel fire. We can only pray they have no wish to harm a child."

"Bastards!" John Jay swore.

Abby looked at Charles. "Go home with your fish and play the happy fisherman. Someone may be watching the house."

Charles scowled for a moment, but knew Abby's plan was a good one. He had complete faith in the Hartnell's Indian servant Andres, who was almost like a member of their family. "Good luck," was all he could say. Then affecting a jaunty walk he went out to his buggy, bid them a smiling farewell and headed for home.

Once they were alone, Abby went into John Jay's arms, tears brimming in her eyes. "They are going to be very sorry they have taken our son," she promised. "Very sorry."

"You're going to give them the fake records?"

"Yes, and pray they won't look past a few Presidential seals," she said.

"And pray that Night Wolf can find Jay."

"He's the only one who could. If we alert the sheriff or the military they would know."

"So what do I do tomorrow while you're in town getting the records?" he asked, feeling helpless.

"Stay home. Find a project to keep you busy, and at times visible so they know you aren't talking to any authorities."

"I can't just sit still…!"

"I know you can't. But you have to…for Jay's sake."

John Jay took his handkerchief and dabbed at the tears in her eyes. "I'd really like to get my hands on them! He's just a child!"

"So would I. We can only hope Night Wolf can do it for us. They won't be expecting that."

Their supper of fresh fish, tamales and beans seemed tasteless when all they could think about was what Jay must be going through with a group of strangers. The boy had a temper. They might find him a handful.

Delfina ate her dinner with Ellie, keeping her occupied while Abby and John Jay grieved for their missing son. It was the only way she could help. Ellie was too young to understand what was happening though she did realize her brother wasn't there.

"Jay Jay?" she asked Delfina. That was their pet name for Jay.

Delfina didn't know what to say. Fortunately Abby and John Jay came into her room just then to kiss her good night.

"Sleep tight, angel," John Jay told his daughter as he did every night.

Before going to their room, John Jay got the

bottle of whisky to help them both sleep. As they were settling into their bed, Abby gave a very unladylike belch. John Jay couldn't help but laugh. Abby rarely touched spirits. She grabbed her pillow and slammed him for laughing. Grabbing his pillow, John Jay fought back. Soon they were laughing, pummeling each other until chicken feathers exploded all around them.

John Jay started picking feathers out of her hair, until he noticed some on her breasts, and began plucking up those too. Abby's laughter turned to something else as she felt his hand on her breast. Playfully she plucked a feather from his chin, then kissed him there.

His lips found hers, and their playfulness had suddenly turned very, very serious. Abby's gown was whisked over her head as she was pushing his pajama bottoms down. They came together, naked, frantic, needing to forget, just for a moment, their worry for their son.

30

The next morning Commissioner Higby was surprised to find a carriage waiting outside his office when he arrived. He started to smile and greet his unexpected visitor until he saw the signs of strain on Abby's pale face.

"Come in. Come in," he said, helping her down from her carriage, surprised to see her alone. Sensing trouble, he hurried to open his office door.

His staff had arrived before him and had coffee ready, as usual, and added an extra cup when they saw he had a visitor.

"Sit, Mrs. Butterfield," he said, knowing she wouldn't speak until the men were gone. He poured coffee for them both.

Abby added a splash of cream before she settled back on the sofa. Higby had taken an easy chair facing her.

"What's happened?" he asked, knowing it would take something major to upset this woman.

"Our son was kidnapped yesterday."

"Kidnapped! Did you call the sheriff?"

Abby handed him the note. Even the Commissioner's face went pale. For a moment he was at a loss for words, then his face brightened. "The fake records?"

Abby nodded. "In the President's satchel. If the security guard, Jenner, is involved in this, he'll know the difference."

The Commissioner nodded. "Over the years I've collected a few records with the Presidents' seal on them. And I faked a few deeper in the stack and added some old surveyor's plats. Unless they look really close, there's a very good chance they won't see the difference."

"Do you think it will fool him?"

"The plats should, they're rather technical and it takes some knowledge to read them. As for the others, they'd have to sit down for a long time and go thru them page by page."

"We can only hope they won't have time for that," Abby said.

"You have a plan," he said, knowing this woman's reputation for resourcefulness.

"I do, but it's best if I don't discuss it." She took

a quick sip of her coffee. "I'll send you word as soon as I can."

"Ma'am, I wish you the best of luck in recovering your son. I just wish I could help."

"You already will once you bring me that satchel."

"Wait here." Commissioner Higby left the office through a side door.

Abby began pacing the room, worry for Jay etched in every line on her face, coffee forgotten.

The Commissioner returned with the Presidential satchel, bulging with records. Abby set it on his desk and opened it, trying to view it as if she were one of the kidnappers, and especially Albert Jenner. She leafed through some pages seeing official documents and the Presidential seal, survey plats and other formal documents mentioning Indians.

"If I didn't know better," she said with a sigh of relief, "I'd think it was the real thing."

"We'll be saying a prayer that they'll be fooled and you'll find your son safe."

"Thank you. Now, if you don't mind, I'm going to sit here for a while and have another cup of coffee. I'm certain I was being followed, and we want them to think I had trouble convincing you to give this up."

The Commissioner nodded as he poured them

both more coffee. Then he asked her about her meeting with President Grant, whom he had met briefly when he was appointed Commissioner of Indian Affairs. He also spoke of his experience with the Northern California Indians, where he had tried to save what land he could for them. It had been an overwhelming task because too many Whites coveted Indian land.

When enough time had passed, he went out with Abby to her waiting carriage, carrying the satchel. He helped her up to the driver's seat and handed her the precious satchel which she stowed under her seat. Then, with a wave to the Commissioner she headed for home.

She wished she knew where Night Wolf was and if he had gotten the message about Jay.

John Jay had been fidgeting, trying to stay busy as he waited for Abby to return, wondering why it was taking so long. When her carriage finally pulled up at the back of the house, he lifted her down, hugging her.

"I was worried," he said.

"We had to make it look as if I had to convince the Commissioner to give up the records," she said softly into his ear. "It's under the seat."

John Jay retrieved the satchel and handed it to

her before he took the horse and carriage into the barn. Abby went into the house. Now they could only wait to be contacted.

The Champion's large two story home sat near the top of a hill that reached from Old Town, where the original Spanish families had settled, toward what was fast becoming down town San Diego. A wide mouthed canyon, filled with old native trees and heavy brush, separated the old and new San Diego. Eventually the canyon opened onto low hills and then flat lands with some ranchos, and now newer families were finding it good land for their crops.

The house Abby and John Jay bought sat on the south side of the canyon in a sparsely populated residential area. The properties were fairly large to accommodate barns and some livestock. Since they came here infrequently, they only required the two horses pulling their largest carriage. Charles and Violet Champion, who also owned a ranch several miles from town had loaned them a horse for their lighter carriage as well as two riding horses.

At the age of four, Jay was fearless, which required constant vigilance from his parents. She wondered how their son was faring with the kidnappers. Were they feeding him? And when would they hear from them?

Delfina was cleaning house to stay busy, yet kept an eye on Ellie, who seemed content playing with her dolls. Though she often asked when her brother was coming home, she didn't understand the seriousness of his absence. Especially since Jay didn't play with dolls, being more interested in riding his saw horse and practicing his roping.

Abby and John Jay didn't speak as they sat at the kitchen table trying to force down their food, and the fresh tea Delfina had made.

A sudden loud bang startled them as something struck the side of the house, and had them on their feet running out the back door.

It took several minutes of searching before John Jay found a rock with a note tied around it with string. Using his pocket knife, John Jay cut the string and carefully unwound the note while Abby waited impatiently. Delfina stood on the back steps, lines of worry on her dark face.

The writing was barely legible. "Mrs. Butterfield. Alone. On horse. Bring satchel up canyon trail and look for sign. No one follow. We watch. Come now."

"No!" John Jay moaned. "I can't let you go alone!"

"You have to. I'm going to change into riding clothes, you saddle the palomino, Jay likes her best."

Abby ran to her room, changed from her day dress to a split riding skirt, a long sleeved blouse, a hat with a chin strap and a kerchief around her neck. As she went through the kitchen, Delfina handed her a canteen and some sandwiches and cookies.

"Bless you," Abby said giving her a quick hug.

John Jay already had the satchel secured behind the saddle, and secured the package of food on top. His face was etched with worry.

"Don't follow me," she warned. "They'll know."

"But I can't just sit here…"

"You have to. We can't risk anything going wrong." Her face softened. "Stay strong, my love. I'll bring him home."

She leaned down for a kiss, then rode out while John Jay could only stand, helpless, and watch her go.

Abby followed the dirt wagon road until it came to the canyon that split the two hills of San Diego. Here, there was only a trail through a thick growth of trees and brush.

The palomino the Champions had loaned them was an alert mare named Daisy. Her ears were perked forward as they listened to bird calls and moved silently along the trail. Abby noted there were many hiding places in the thick undergrowth. Her gaze moving constantly in search of the next contact. She also watched Daisy's ears. They would alert her to anything unusual.

If she was going to be told where to go, it would be soon. The canyon was only about five miles long, then it opened out onto flatlands with scattered farms.

Rounding a thick growth of brush, Aby spotted a note nailed to a tree just ahead. She watched Daisy's ears, but she didn't seem to hear any sounds to alert her. Looking around carefully, Abby knew they had to be watching this spot. Half way up the north side of the canyon, she caught the reflection of a spyglass or binoculars but pretended not to notice. She took the note from the tree and unfolded it.

"Twenty feet ahead, take narrow track north," it read.

As they moved on, Daisy's ears began moving constantly. She was picking up sounds but not certain where from.

Abby found the narrow track and turned into the heavy brush seeing other horse tracks. She hadn't gone far when she heard a sound behind her and reined Daisy to a stop.

"Don't turn around!" a male voice ordered. "And don't make a move."

She could hear someone walking up behind her and felt the presence of others nearby. "Where's my son?" she demanded.

"He's close. You just do as I say and you'll have him back," the voice was closer now. "Reach behind you and free the satchel. Don't turn around."

It was awkward to do it by feel, but Abby took the pack of food first and placed it in front of her on the saddle. She then freed the straps holding the satchel and let it fall to the ground.

Daisy danced nervously, not liking the sound of the man behind her.

"Keep going on this trail," the man ordered. "At the big oak there'll be a barely visible trail to your right. You'll find the boy there."

Abby urged Daisy forward, eager to retrieve her son. At the giant oak she saw the narrow track, barely wide enough for a horse. She was saying prayers in both Kumeyaay and English that her son was safe. The heavy brush slapped at Daisy and Abby's legs but she could tell by Daisy's ears that she could hear something ahead.

31

Night Wolf had shadowed Abby on foot from the moment she entered the canyon. His moccasins made no sound and he stayed far enough behind that he could hear any other noises.

He had heard the man's approach when he had stepped out onto the trail behind Abby and called out to her. Seeing no immediate danger to Abby, he waited as she complied with the man's demands and untied the satchel, letting it drop to the ground. And he heard the man telling her where to find her son.

He gave a soft bird call to alert his men scattered in the brush behind him, then when the man vanished into the brush with the satchel, he followed.

Hidden in the deep brush the man had a horse,

mounted it, hooking the satchel straps over his saddle horn, and followed a narrow animal trail toward the north side of the canyon.

Since the man moved slowly, Night wolf was able to stay behind him, occasionally giving a bird call for his warriors. Their calls were not the only animal sounds in this dense undergrowth, so they didn't fear the men recognizing their communication.

Hoping to confront the kidnappers, Night Wolf and his followers had dressed as warriors of earlier days; loin cloths, deer skin vests that left most of their chests bared, and beaded headbands to hold back their long black hair, some with eagle feathers. He was glad they had chosen rifles for this pursuit rather than bows and arrows or spears. Plus each man had a long-bladed hunting knife.

In the distance behind them, Night Wolf knew Andres was leading a small band of soldiers and listening for Night Wolf's whistles.

The man he was following led Night Wolf to an opening, where a wide ring had been cleared of brush, and one man stepped forward to take the satchel. He was wearing an Eastern looking suit, so Night Wolf guessed this man was the leader, the one from Washington D.C. He almost held his breath as the man opened the satchel and began to leaf through the contents.

A new, different bird call from Night Wolf didn't arouse any suspicions among the men, two of whom held rifles and watched for any signs of pursuit.

Seemingly satisfied with what he saw, the leader carried the satchel to the cleared area and emptied its contents onto the ground. Papers with the Presidential seal and survey plats fluttered out. From his pocket, the leader took a box of safety matches.

There was a big smile on the man's face as he struck a match and held it to one corner of a document. As it began to burn he set three more documents ablaze.

"Well done boys," Jenner said. "This will set them back long enough for our men in Washington to get these nullified."

"Think she'll find the boy?" one ventured.

"I don't care if she does or not. We got what we came for."

There was barely a sound to alert him but Jenner suddenly felt the hairs on the back of his neck stand up. Looking across the now blazing fire, he saw an Indian warrior with a rifle pointed right at him.

A movement to his right drew his attention to another warrior, then another, and another. They were surrounded.

"Drop your rifles!" Night Wolf ordered.

Realizing they were surrounded by well-armed savages, the men dropped their weapons, their faces going pasty white with fear.

"You're too late," Jenner gloated. "There's your reservations." He pointed at the fire.

Night Wolf gave a loud piercing whistle that would carry to Andres and the waiting soldiers. He didn't want to tell the men they'd burned the wrong records. It was better if they thought their plan had succeeded.

With the kidnappers disarmed and another whistle to guide Andres to their location, he left his men to guard them and went on the run to find Abby and her son.

Abby's fears grew as she neared the mouth of the canyon and she'd seen no signs to guide her to her son. It took all her will power not to panic.

"Jason!" she shouted. Her only answer was the sound of the breeze through the trees and an occasional bird call.

What if they never intended for her to find him?

Drawing Daisy to a stop, she watched the horse's ears. They were working back and forth but she wasn't tracking any particular sounds. Turning to look behind her, her sharp gaze searched the trees and brush for any signs left by the kidnappers. She knew she wouldn't have missed it.

Help. She needed help.

In the past, she had rarely called on her spirit guide, the golden eagle, but more than once one had showed up to warn her of danger or sent her a vision. Closing her eyes, she cleared her mind and pictured an eagle as if drawing it to her.

Only silence, the soft breeze. No sound of a small boy's voice. It was all she could do to keep from wailing out loud. Jay, where are you, her mind called.

Many long minutes passed, but then she heard it, from behind her, the high pitched screech of a golden eagle. She turned Daisy around, trying to pin point the sound. It came again. And, ahead of her, off to the left, she caught a glimpse of an eagle circling above a section of heavy brush. The large female gave another loud cry, circled again, and then vanished over the rim of the canyon.

"Jay!" she called "Jason! Where are you?"

Daisy was fully alert now and intent on one area as she stepped faster.

"Mama! Mama!" a voice called.

Moments later Abby tumbled off Daisy and ran

to her son, tied to a tree. Hugging and crying they both gave vent to their relief.

"I called and called for you!" he wailed. "They said you would come." He was gasping and sobbing, trying to explain. "I called! I cried! But I fell asleep."

"Oh, baby," she sobbed as she took her hunting knife from her boot and cut him loose.

"I saw this big bird!" he choked as he went into her arms. "I think it woke me."

"Yes, she led me to you."

"Was it one of the birds from the ranch?" he asked, wiping away his tears.

"I don't know," Abby said. "But wherever she came from, she led me to you."

A sudden movement on the trail brought an alarmed snort from Daisy and brought Abby's knife up in defense. She could hardly believe the sight of a warrior of old. Night Wolf, looking much as he had many years ago. With a sigh of relief she returned the knife to her boot.

"I followed the cry of the eagle," he said. "I knew she would bring me to you. I'm glad your son is safe."

"But..." she motioned to his warrior dress. "What?"

"We knew it would scare those men more than

anything else would," he said with a grin.

"You found them?"

"Yes. They were burning your papers. We surrounded them, then called in Andres and some soldiers."

Abby smiled in relief. "Did you tell them what they had burned?"

"No, we decided not to. We want them to think they were successful, so they won't try again."

"Good idea," she said.

A loud nicker from Daisy drew their attention to the crashing sound of a horse moving swiftly through the narrow trail toward them.

Night Wolf turned to face the intruder, but Daisy's call was one of recognition. A horse came out of the brush.

"John Jay!" Abby cried as he tumbled from his saddle into a frantic embrace of his wife and son. He was crying as he held them, savoring the fact they were both alive and well. After a moment, he reached out a hand to clasp Night Wolf's in thanks.

32

August 1876
   Dear John Jay and Abby,
      Things went crazy in the aftermath of the Custer tragedy. In spite of President Grant's pleas for calm, efforts against Sitting Bull and his people have been stepped up. Rumor has it he has fled to Canada.

The Lakota and the Cheyenne have been pursued ruthlessly. Even agency Indians who had remained loyal have been made to surrender their horses and their guns.

New forts are being built and buffalo are being slaughtered so the Indians won't have their main food source. They'll have no choice but to accept the government's hand outs and stay on the reservations.

But, brother, I knew George Custer. I've read the classified reports on what happened to him and can't help thinking he was partly to blame.

He thought of himself as a great Indian fighter,

and by attacking the village ahead of Reno and Benteen, he would be the hero of the day. I wouldn't be surprised if part of the reason for all his dispatches to the newspapers over the years was with a secret goal in mind. Custer wanted to be president.

Instead, he has heaped terrible destruction on all Indians.

I am glad your California Indians are mostly untouched by this tragedy, and that you and your medicine woman are helping those in your area.

Let me know if I can do anything to help, though this would not be a good time to remind our government officials about California.

And President Grant was smart to rush those reservations out of D.C. before the news about Custer hit his Cabinet and Congress. One of their first reactions was to try to call them back. But it was too late.

Mother and Julia send their love. We all miss you.

Regards,
Daniel

33

The sound of many drums filled the deepening twilight. Flutes, chanting, gourd rattles, and both men and women dancing around numerous fires brought a happy smile to Abby's lips as she rested in the shadows of an old oak tree. It was a celebration of the nine clans whose reservations were now confirmed by President Grant. This area was called Campo, and it was the only area large enough to hold so many clans at one time. Each group had set up its own sleeping area with tents or teepees. Food was shared at many fires. Old friendships were renewed, new ones formed.

The last time Abby had seen John Jay, he was with a group of fathers playing games with the young boys. Their own children they had left at home with Cita, their new helper, while Delfina was here celebrating with her clan.

Indian Commissioner Higby and the head surveyor, Jake Wilcox, had set up a large tent where they presented the Head Elders of each clan with the official document of their reservation earlier that day.

Now was the time to celebrate with a great fiesta that Abby knew would go on for days. Some gatherings were called Pow Wows. But this impromptu one was a fiesta.

Gathered here were families from Santa Ysabel, Capitan Grande, La Jolla, Pala, Sycuan, Rincon, Los Coyotes, Cuyapaipe and Viejas, and Abby was proud to have had a part in making this gathering possible.

A man she didn't recognize sought her out and spoke to her in a Kumeyaay dialect that she could tell wasn't his first language. He was a tall, middle-aged warrior of the type she rarely saw any more with his well-muscled bare chest.

"Your husband, he say come." He indicated an area in the trees.

"What is he doing out there?" she asked half to herself because the tall man had already turned and strode toward the nearest fire.

It didn't dawn on her until she was in the deep

shadows of the trees that something was amiss. She heard a horse snorting and stamping its feet nervously, and, as her eyes adjusted to the gloom, she saw a horse whose head was being held by a large Indian.

"Abby! Go back!" came her husband's warning as she realized the man on the horse's back was her husband. His hands were tied behind his back, and a noose was around his neck.

The warrior's laughter told her it was Sotero, his disfigured face barely visible in the gloom. Once he was certain of Abby's attention, he pulled the horse forward until John Jay was left hanging by the rope.

"John Jay!" she screamed as she ran to him, trying to keep him from being choked to death. The gagging sound made her frantic as she stood under him, placing each of his boots on her shoulders to ease the strain on his neck.

Sotero howled with laughter at her attempt to save her husband. It would do her no good to call for help. The pounding of drums and chanting were too loud.

Abby struggled to keep John Jay balanced, and the strain off his neck.

Sotero pulled a long bladed knife from a sheath

and stuck it in the ground about twenty feet from Abby. "Here, Eagle Woman, use this to cut him down. I go for whiskey. When I come back he will be dead. You will not save him. Then I come for you." His grin was pure evil. "And then I go for your whelps."

Too stunned by his words to speak, Abby now faced the additional threat to her children.

John Jay tried to speak but the rope about his neck was too tight, he gagged and struggled for breath. Frantically Abby looked for help, someone near enough to hear her call out, but Sotero had chosen this spot well. No one would hear her. The knife he left taunted her. She'd never get it and climb the tree to cut the rope before her husband was strangled to death.

Then she spotted several horses grazing among the trees. One looked like Brian Carter's horse Rosie. She tried to imitate Brian's whistle but her mouth was so dry it took three tries before Rosie raised her head. She looked around for Brian, not seeing him, but followed the sound to find the strange sight of John Jay balancing on Abby's shoulders.

"Come Rosie," Abby urged, but the mare was too confused, her ears flicking this way and that as she looked for Brian.

Abby felt her strength draining away. She couldn't hold her husband much longer.

Then suddenly Brian was at Rosie's head. "Rosie, what…" he broke off when he saw the scene before him. He knew at once what he had to do and led Rosie to Abby, and between them they switched John Jay onto her back.

At the easing of the rope around his neck John Jay was drawing in great breaths of air.

Abby dashed to the knife Sotero had left to taunt her and scrambled up the oak tree to the limb where the rope was tied. Stretching out flat on the limb she could reach the rope and sawed thru it.

John Jay collapsed onto Rosie's withers, gasping. A moment later Abby was hugging him and cutting away the noose.

"Sotero?" Brian asked. "I thought I saw him earlier, always in the shadows."

"Yes," her eyes were flashing with fire as she stroked Rosie's nose. "Take John Jay to Delfina, she will know how to treat the rope burns."

"No, Abby," John Jay rasped.

"He has threatened our babies," she said angrily. "I must deal with him now!" She nodded to

Brian to take him. Too weak to argue, John Jay clung to Rosie's mane as Brian led her away.

For a moment she was grateful her husband was safe, then she searched the ground for just the right chunk of wood and sat on a fallen oak. Using Sotero's knife, she began to whittle, and the figure of an eagle began to take shape.

He came out of the darkness, staggering drunkenly, another long bladed knife in his hand. He stared in disbelief to the spot where John Jay should have been hanging, and hopefully the Eagle Woman would be collapsed in grief under his body. Instead she was sitting on a fallen tree, whittling.

"No!" he screamed. "Where is he?"

"Safe," Abby said, alert now to his every move. At this moment he was more dangerous than an angry rattlesnake.

"How could you have…?" He gave a loud bellow of rage and charged, his knife raised over his head for a deadly strike.

Abby barely had time to turn her knife around and thrust it out in protection. Sotero blundered into the blade that pierced his stomach…bringing him up short. Unbelievingly he stared down at the blood gushing from his stomach, then at Abby. His knife slipped from his suddenly weak hands.

"You tried to kill my man and you have threatened my babies," Abby's green eyes were burning like fire in the darkness.

With a cry of horror and anguish, Sotero turned and staggered off into the night.

The sound of voices alerted Abby to the arrival of Brian and several Kumeyaay men armed with rifles, one of them her brother Weatuk.

"Where is he?" Brian asked, seeing two knives on the ground, one covered in blood.

"That way," Abby pointed, suddenly feeling drained of energy and worried about her husband.

The Indians charged off in the direction Abby pointed, and Brian stayed behind to help her back to her tent.

"Your husband will be okay," Brian assured her. "He'll just have a sore throat for a while. Weatuk and his friends will make certain Sotero won't threaten you again."

When they reached her tent, he left her, as Abby rushed inside and into John Jay's waiting arms, tears streamed down her cheeks. Tears of relief that he was safe, tears that she had been forced to kill to protect her family.

Weatuk and the other men came back with the news they had found Sotero dead in the forest, and had left his body for the scavengers. He didn't deserve a ritual burial.

With that news, Sotero's cohorts and their whiskey vanished into the night.

The celebration of the new reservations went on for hours, drumming and chanting and dancing, while in their tent, John Jay and Abby shared the oldest ritual of all. The ritual of love.

EPILOGUE

The writing of this sequel was far more difficult than I expected. Trying to make sense of what was happening to the indigenous people of California was a daunting task.

Nothing was truly settled for the tribes until well into the 1900s. The missing treaties sent to Washington D.C. were not located until 1923. Misfiled! By the time the reservations were finally assigned, many of the Native Americans had moved off tribal land to take jobs or starve. Where they had once been able to travel to their food sources throughout the year, now they were confined to some areas so small or so rocky they were unable to grow crops.

San Diego County alone has nineteen reservations. Today, there are many casinos on the larger reservations, with monies being spent to improve conditions for even the smaller ones. And they are educating their men and women to handle the tribes' affairs.

In the time period of my story, Indians were not permitted to attend White schools, and could not bring criminal charges against a White man.

To me, the time period of my story was a shameful one for a people who had lived mostly peacefully on their lands for thousands of years. But on the Plains, as more and more whites encroached on Indian land, there was much violence.

Helen Hunt Jackson, in the late 1800s was like a lone voice trying to awaken Americans to the shameful way the indigenous tribes were being treated, all over the continent, not just California.

I have tried to recreate a history both uplifting as well as factual. There were those individuals working for the welfare of the tribes as well as those all too eager to steal their land.

Even once reservations had been assigned, the government kept full control, thinking the Native Americans too ignorant to handle their own affairs or their money, a lot of which managed to disappear.

But once educated, the people took back control of their sovereign lands, formed their own law enforcement, and their own government.

As a white person, I can't possibly fully understand the wrongs these people endured, but I am proud to say they persevered. They have taken their place outside of the reservation in every walk of life and continue to fight for justice.

I hope you have enjoyed this glimpse into a very colorful period in our nation's history, and the people I have created to bring the story to life.

ABOUT THE AUTHOR

Marian Sepulveda's compulsion to write began in the seventh grade in the late 1940s, when Western movies were all the rage. Her interest expanded to Science Fiction when it became popular in the early years of television. Even as an adult working for General Telephone Company she never stopped writing. By  then, romance novels were all the rage, and she wrote many. Unpublished, though she had much encouragement from the editors.

Marian always had a love of early California history and animals. Her pets ranged from dogs and cats to a ferret, a bobcat, gopher snake, and various birds from parakeets to parrots. In the early 1970s she moved to the desert in the Coach-ella Valley of Southern California. There she met the man who became her husband, Steve Sepul-veda. She became fascinated by his ancestors, who migrated from Sepulveda, Spain, to Mexico, and then California. They arrived at the Spanish presidio of San Diego in 1781. It is their story she hopes will be her next project.

Marian and Steve shared many traveling adven-tures, preferring the wild places outdoors, four-wheeling into remote canyons. It was on a trip to Tombstone Arizona they met artist Marjorie Reed, whose life work was to paint every stage stop of the Butterfield Overland Mail. Marjorie generously gave the couple five books she had published of her paintings. And that began Marian's fascina-tion with Butterfield history, which became part of Where Eagles Dance, the first novel of the saga.

In the early 1990s, after Marian retired from the phone company, she and Steve became docents at the Living Desert Zoo and Botanical Gardens in Palm Desert. The zoos outdoor habitats were home to many desert creatures from big horn sheep to birds of prey, even two non-releasable golden eagles. Marian trained to handle certain of the animals so she could introduce them to visitors, up close and very personal. And still, she was writing in her spare time.

Marian lost Steve to Alzheimer's in 1993, and lost her desire to write. She continued to work at The Living Desert. She wanted to be outdoors, not tied to a desk. The animals and nature sustained her. Then, years later, a friend challenged her to embrace her muse. So Marian picked up the unfinished manuscript of "Where Eagles Dance" and went back to work. This was a story that insisted on being told. And the response by readers took her totally by surprise. After years of rejection slips, people were raving about her book. And wanted more.

In between, Marian wrote a novel based in part on her experiences at The Living Desert, which she called Desert World. Available only as an ebook through Amazon Kindle, you will meet two adorable mountain lion kittens and a wily raven, among others. A story of romance and intrigue at the zoo.

Eagle Woman was not part of the plan until readers asked for more, and it has been a real challenge to put it together.

Marian says, "I hope you'll enjoy reading these stories as much as I will enjoy bringing them to you."

Share your comments with author Marian Sepulveda:
WhereEaglesDance@gmail.com

Did you enjoy reading *Eagle Woman*? Please be sure to check out Marian Sepulveda's other novels at amazon.com.